Praise for I

'Peasants, bailiffs, myths and muck, *Mother Naked* has the lot. This is the kind of novel we should be seeing more of. Daring and original. It's a work of speculative fiction. A historical re-enactment. A howl against the injustices of class. But above all it is absolutely teeming with voice as the dark ages are sprung back to life.'

—James Clarke, author of *Sanderson's Isle*

Praise for Ironopolis

'When the literary depiction of working-class communities is often reduced to a lazy shorthand of grit and misery, this unflinching, clear-eyed and overall deeply human depiction of an estate's glory days and its eventual decline is nothing short of a triumph.'

—Kerry Hudson, *Guardian*

'An unflinching tale about narratives at the heart of working class communities and the struggle to keep them alive.'

—*Northern Soul*

'The most accomplished working class novel of the last few years.'

—*The Morning Star*

A catalogue record for this book is available
from the British Library

First published in 2024 by Peninsula Press
400 Kingsland Road
E8 4AA
London

peninsulapress.co.uk

Cover design by gray318
Typesetting by Francisca Monteiro

Printed in Great Britain by CPI Group (UK) Ltd, Croydon

2 4 6 8 10 9 7 5 3 1

ISBN-13: 9781913512484

Mother
Naked

Glen James
Brown

PENINSULA PRESS, LONDON

To my parents John and Jaqueline Brown. And my sister, Lauren.
And to Modyr Nakett.

The 1433-1434 ledger of the Bursar of Durham Priory recorded all payments into and out of the cathedral, including money spent on entertainment. Among the many performers that year, there was a single reference to one called *Modyr Nakett:* Mother Naked.

Mother Naked received one groat (four pence) for their act. This was the lowest payment to any performer in over two hundred years of surviving records.

f riends! On this feast of Saint Godric, I must first say one thing. To the reverend Sacrist, his two esteemed guests at the head table, and all else gathered in this hall—I cry pardon. Shamed, I be, by the tardiness of the hour, and my sodden state. For the storm that still howls now at these glass casements did wet me through on my walk to Durham this day, and then, when following the Clerk's directions to the nearest warm hearth, I cloddishly became waylaid once more. Lost as I was some tyme afore a Monk found me in the cellars, amid the kegs of wine and ale ye all now sup. But I took no drynke myself. No wine shall pass mine lips 'til my task here be ended. Though, Sacrist, I pray the fine claret hath cushioned thine guests' long wait for the evening's entertainment.

Of which, friends, I bear ill news. Mayhap the Sacrist hath already noised to all here the message I relayed to his Clerk. That, alas, I be not the Gleeman Melchior Blanchfl—

...Friends!...

...*FRIENDS*! Ye be angered, aye, but hush as I tell of the particulars!...

...I thank you all for the silence. The truth be Melchior Blanchflower, that legendary Gleeman who was once part of the fifth King Henry's court, and who was due to perform for ye this night, he hath been lain low by a sudden malady. In dede, I was with him this morning at Finchale Priory, when the pestilence struck so savagely—so swiftly—that it left the man unable even to hold a quill and provide word of his own situation. Instead, he bade me relay a message, which I do now. I quoth the man from memory.

To the Sacrist of Durham cathedral, his Cellarer, Master Mercer, and all attendant Mercery guild members—greetings from Melchior Blanchflower. Friends, I have travelled plenteous miles from the noble de Colton court of Westmorland, so that I might weave songs and tales for your exalted company. Yet I am thwarted almost within sight of Durham's city walls. Aye, this regret shall be carried upon my funeral briar, alongside my corpse! As such, apology will not suffice— I must redress. Grant me leave, then, to offer my peer and friend in my stead. This man now speaking mine words is a Gleeman of long-standing and great skill. And though his psaltery is old and battered, the strings of that musical instrument coax the very birds from their boughs. So, I bid you all—venerate Mother Naked as you would me.

Aye, friends, your laughter sounds familiar. My name be strange, but I shall reveal its meaning in tyme. First, though, I thank dear Melchior! His praise be o'erkind! And while he speaks true of my ability, unlike him I was never attach't to a noble house like that of the de Colton, much less the court of the King! For this reason, I cannot repeat Melchior's tales of daring that make him a famous man in every corner of England.

For he, not I, was with King Henry during the Siege of Meaux.

He, not I, saw Charles the Mad vanquish't at Harfleur.

And he, not I, trod the misted fields of Agincourt and Rouen.

Those tales be Melchior's, and would sound false upon my own tongue. Thus, I be compelled to tell a different story.

But what could *possibly* rival warring 'twixt Kings?

Friends, I believe I know. My story takes place much closer to hame than the blood-stomp't battlefields of France. Actually, it unravelled right here, scant miles beyond Durham's city walls...

...The sorrowful, tragic tale of the *Fell Wraith*...

...Ah, judging by your faces, I see the name be known to some! Yet for those still in befuddlement, this dread creature goes by other titles. At Raby, they whisper of the *Red Rape*. In Monkwearmuthe, the *Jigging Ghost*. Cestria speaks of *Brok-Armed Annie*. And only this past year, I heard a Priest in Shildon make this same monster the theme of his lesson after Mass, relaying the tale of the *Segerston Wraith* to his quaking parishioners. Segerston, said he, was a wicked village of idlers punish't by that undead fiend for its slothful denial of God, and was thus struck down...

...The crops *putrefied*...

...The manor house *burn't* to cinders...

...And the villagers *butchered* or else driven to frenzy, their minds *smash't* forever...

...Aye, friends, Segerston was near razed from the Earth. And it just occurs that Segerston was one of thine manors, Sacrist, be that true? Aye, I thought so. And though the Fell Wraith's name changes from town to town, the tale—the terror—remains the same. And where terror goes, balladry follows. Take this song I learn't from a Gleeman in Jarrow. Allow me to strum my psaltery in accompaniment—

> *In heath and in gorse, barefoot moves she,*
> *Gleeful 'neath moonlight her terrible sallies.*
> *For those whom misfortune bade them to see,*
> *The crop-rotted fields her pestilence harries.*
> *All life into death,*
> *All death into fern.*
> *Dance with her shadow,*
> *As thy own manor burns...*

...Friends, forgive the crudeness of verse! This doggerel be composed by rustics for rustics, so must grate your rare ears to hear. I sing it only to shew that, though dead, this creature—this rotting, walking ghost—be still very much alive in these Durham lands.

I acquired this knowledge at great cost to myself. As ye can see, I be an auld man of almost fifty. How much more tyme God grants me, I know not. Thus, I wish unburden myself of this story afore I die. Ye, wise friends, seem the perfect men to receive it.

But at yonder head table, the Sacrist now confers with his two special guests. Ye younger men feasting this night, ye might not recognise the eminent silver-haired fellow now in deep discussion with our host, but that be the Sacrist's former Cellarer—once o'erseer of his manors. And as for the other man, well, I *hardly* need introduce Walter Attwell, the Sacrist's own Master Mercer, and elder of thy very own Mercer guild!

Aye, friends, there be much consternation 'twixt the three of them, the subject of which I can guess upon, so, Sacrist, if I may address thee direct—let me say I do not open auld wounds for mere frippery. What I tell be no base ghost story fit only for the frightening of bairns. There be a grander purpose, Sacrist, one you shall see in goode tyme. And look, the rain redoubles at the glass, and thine guests grow restless for entertainment. I shall speak to them—friends, do ye wish hear this terrible tale...?

...Aye, raise up your voices!...

...Sacrist, hear the cries of these Mercers! Three dozen men as parch't for a story as for the wine and ale in their cups! And who can slake that thirst, if not me...?

...Thank thee, Sacrist. Thy faith in me shall be repaid. Now, with official consent granted, I beseech you, friends, refill your cups and settle down. I wish no man here to miss a word of what I say, for I assure it shall change thee evermore. And with a tuning of my psaltery's strings, we begin—

This bloody tale we now shall wend,
From harrowed start to grievous end...

2

...But
was what that Shildon Priest said of Segerston true? *Was* it a
sloven place whose rustics refused to work the land, and thus
deserved the Wraith's bloody wrath? Friends, I see many Mercer
brows furrowing at what I say. Ye be thinking—*how can a rustic
reject land?* After all, God *made* them for fieldwork, did he not?
Well, a description of rustic lyf in those dim days may grant
comprehension, for much hath changed 'twixt then and now.
This lesson be especially important for you younger Mercers—
for ye were born into the new way of things and might not
know that, forty years ago, rustics did not possess the liberties
they flaunt in these modern tymes. And why *should* ye know it?
Why should important men be expected to grasp the affairs of
rural lowborns from afore ye even suckled the teat?

At this poynte, allow me to introduce my friend Pearl Eye
into our tale. Like myself, Pearl was a wandering Gleeman and
my auld touring partner of many decades. His queer name
was due to his milky and blind left orb, yet the man witness't
more with one eye than most do with two. And so it was Pearl
once pass't through Segerston at the tyme our tale be set—in
1396—scant months afore the Fell Wraith brought murder to
the place...

3

...As he telt it, the day was the 23rd of June—the
feast of Saint John. Pearl was going south to Derlyngton, for

the July fayre held there, when, upon a whim, he bore south-west at Cestria along a minor road leading to Segerston. The village perch't like a clutch of buzzard eggs upon a steep and elevated heugh of land, and though the sky was low-clouded, this height granted Pearl the sight of Saint John bonefyres being lit northwards across the land almost to Newcastle.

As we all know, Saint John's towering fyres and feasting ought be a joyous occasion. But Pearl said Segerston that night was sombre. Many acres of wasted lands did he witness, choke't with mud and weeds; the crumbling, empty cottages of the dead strip't of timbers and iron nail by those still living. These souls, Pearl found in the heart of Segerston; folk devoid of gaiety as they lit their sodden bonefyres. Those of you white of whisker may recall the summer stormings of 1396— deluges to rival Noah's flood, which wash't away crops all across Durham. In dede, on his way into Segerston, Pearl saw hundreds of furloughs of rain-flattened wheat. The prospect of a ruined harvest had likewise flattened the spirits of the villag- ers, huddled 'neath the common green oak, picking at a feast table of scant provision...

A sorry Saint John's, was how Pearl Eye described it to me. The sorriest I ever witness't. Thus I tarried some and played, for to lift their guttered moods.

So play Pearl did. And it comforts me that at least once in their hard, short lives, those rustics saw true greatness. See, I travelled with Pearl many years afore he died, and while I have long since tired of the routines of other Gleemen, with Pearl it was as if each tyme he strummed, the song was born anew. All who heard him play, they felt it *here*, sirs—deep in their breasts. And try as I might, I have never been able to replicate that feeling myself.

9

Yet even Pearl struggled to cheer those Segerston rustics that night, for their worries clung to them like thickest pitch. So that he might redouble his efforts to merry, Pearl took a cup of ale and went to warm himself as close to a damp, smoking bonefyre as he might get without swooning. And it was while gazing into the crackling pyre that he notice't the boy. Not ten years auld, Pearl telt me. Lurking at the threshold of heat and light.

Come closer, said Pearl to him.

Warily, like a leveret emerging from its warren to take its first sneckful of air above ground, the lad did. He crept nearer, the polish't stones of his eyes fix't upon the psaltery lying 'twixt them.

Take it up, said Pearl.

Again, the lad did.

Friends, it was the very psaltery I now hold in mine hands. See its age, the scars wrought upon the frame. But see, too, the exquisite workmanship, the intricate carvings and channels once inlaid with gold. This instrument hath a long and sorrowful history, which Pearl thought sounded in the very notes it made. And he telt me he detected some glimmer of that understanding in the lad's eyes as he turned the instrument in his hands. Then, just as Pearl was about to instruct him which strings to pluck in harmony, the boy strummed the most mellifluous stream of notes into the night. When they faded, he turned to Pearl Eye, apprehensive of the Gleeman's judgment.

A natural, said Pearl.

The lad's smile faded as had the notes.

Ask't Pearl, *What troubles thee, lad?*

The childe's fingers lay against the psaltery strings.

How might I become a Gleeman?

That, said Pearl, *be a question with many answers. Tell me, lad, be you a freeman?*

Nay, villein.

Pearl sighed. *Then I deliver ill news. Gleemen must be free to wander place to place. A villein be unfree and cannot leave the manor without his Lord's blessing, or else pay him a purse to purchase his freedom.*

How much, the purse?

Princely, said Pearl.

Now the boy sighed. He held the psaltery up to the bonefyre, inspecting the way the strings slice't blackly the flames there.

I thought so, said he. *Father Bell says we villeins be born upon the Lord Sacrist's manor, and shall die here. He says we must first work the Sacrist's demesne lands to profit, and only once that task be done, can we tend our own holdings with whatever tyme remains.*

Father Bell be Segerston's Priest?

The boy nodded.

Pearl sip't his ale. *Then Father Bell speaks true.*

He—Pearl Eye—telt me he wish't he could swallow back those words. Not because they were lies, for they were not. Nay, he simply did not want to crush the boy's spirit any further by speaking of his slim prospects to attain his freedom. Seeing the lad's melancholy expression, the Gleeman offered another solution.

Mayhap you could flee? ask't Pearl. *Did you know if you remain away from thy manor, uncaptured, for one year and one day, you become a freeman by law?*

Nervous, the boy look't about himself, in search of eavesdroppers.

Fleeing be an evil thing, the childe said. *All say that.*

11

Why do they say so?

For when a villein flees, his work must be done by those who stay.

Then I cry pardon for speaking it, said Pearl. *Thy heart be true, lad. You do not seek to escape thy shackles by putting them onto thy neighbour.*

The boy said naught, though his mucky fingers never stop't stroking the psaltery.

Go on, said Pearl. *Play again.*

Fresh notes fluted into the night. This tyme, the lad sang an accompanying melody—soaring like a hawk high o'er the snapping flames. Fain stunned, Pearl listened until the childe finish't and look't once more for the Gleeman's comment. Pearl telt me he agonised whether to speak his mind, for given the boy's villein status it might hurt more than help. But speak it he did.

Childe, said Pearl, *though you must work the Lord Sacrist's acres thy lyf entire, know that you also stand at the summit of a mountain most clamber their whole lives only to be buried at its foot. In dede, many know not which mountain to climb, and so waste their years tackling a false peak.*

Seeing confusion upon the childe's face, Pearl clarified his remark.

Most die without ever knowing what they were goode at.

Like who? ask't the boy.

Like the brewer of this ale, said Pearl, taking a final grimacing sip afore tossing the nasty liquid into the fyre. The boy stood to leave but Pearl bade him halt.

What be thy name, lad?

Payne, said he...

4

...The Payne family. The principal char-
acters of this bitter tale. Friends, does the name chime your
wits? For in some tales of the Fell Wraith's slaughter, the
Paynes be named amongst the monster's victims. Alice Payne
was wyf to the villein Henry Payne, and together they had four
bairns, though only the eldest lad and the youngest—the boy
Pearl spoke with at the bonefyre—still drew breath. Together,
they lived in a cottage rented from thee, Sacrist. One with a toft
and outhouse in front, and a croft of crops in back. Two oxen
they owned, and a dray horse. Pigs, chickens, capons. From and
of these things, the Paynes scratch't at survival.

Their private holdings were a scant twenty acres, split into
furloughs amid the three one-hundred-acre open fields. Twenty
acres was scarcely enough to furnish the Paynes with enough
to eat, sell, and sow the following year; and the labour obligations owed to work the Lord Sacrist's demesne—to plough and
sow it, to harrow and harvest—reduce't still further the tyme
available to tend their own crops. Each day when they were
not expected to work for the Sacrist, Henry and his eldest lad—
some tales give his name as Christopher—work't their own
acres 'til it was too dark to see, and their backs screamed agony.

At night, their work finally done, Henry and Alice would
whisper together upon their sleeping pallet, fretting o'er the
summer rains of 1396, and what it meant for the harvest. Privation was an unwelcome neighbour to rustics then, and the
Paynes knew a failed reap would cast many into vagabondage
—beggars drifting through hamlets, pleading for crusts, their

rag-clad corpses found in some ditch, snufft out by starvation and elemental exposure.

So, worried Henry and Alice Payne—would that?

No doubt it was this question which inspired Alice to brew ale as means of bringing in more coin. With her youngest boy's help, Alice malted a sack of wheat. She then ground the grains at the Lord Sacrist's mill, afore mashing, drawing, and fermenting the wort. There be something alchemical to the production of ale—the transformation of one fundamental into another—and to Alice's delight, she found she had a sure touch when, a week later, there stood in her hame a barrel of delicious, sweet, foamy ale...

5

...But what of it, eh? What of it? Friends, I see it plain on your faces, ye all be thinking—*why does this doltish Gleeman speak of ale?* Be this a *woman's* tale? When do the *guts* start flying? Well, we shall arrive at the steaming viscera directly, for Alice Payne was not the only brewer in Segerston. The other was Joan Deepslough. Like Alice, Joan was a villein woman, but married to a blunt villein man named Ralf, her partner in both bed and certain Wraith songs, such as the following—

> *First sicken grain, then sicken man,*
> *Both of them dying back to the loam.*
> *Yet still be buried according God's plan,*
> *As she had not, thus did she roam.*
> *Hark! Hark! Segerston cries!*

Help us! howled Stephen,
Forgive me! wept John,
I be weak! whispered William, and dying anon.
I beg thee! cried Ralf,
Spare us! begged Joan,
Nay, nay, nay, came the Fell Wraith's dread groan...

...Afore the Wraith came for them, the Deepsloughs were amongst the more prosperous villeins in Segerston. Ralf had inherited some sixty acres from his father, and had, during his own tyme, added double that as collateral upon loans others could not repay him. Such an amount of land would be a crippling burden to most villeins, but Ralf had three stronge sons of age to work it to surplus. This gave Ralf ambition, which in some men does result in arrogance.

Mayhap this was why his wyf, Joan Deepslough, had for some years task't herself with one of Segerston's most important services—brewing the ale. Doing so offered obvious prestige, but also less apparent benefits because her hame became the tavern *de facto*, the centre of supping and idle chatter. It was thus Joan's privilege to be within earshot when ale-loose tongues spill't their gossips, while also granting her perfect opportunity to noise about certain rumours of her own.

But alas, Joan's problem was the taste of her ale—like a Frenchman's bathwater. Mayhap, it was some issue with her malting? Or her barrel had once held some repugnant substance, the residue of which still clung to the wood? Whatever the culprit, the disagreeable brew haunted the gob long after it went down the gullet, as it had Pearl's when he flung the foaming filth into that Saint John bonefyre.

Having endured Joan Deepslough's foul concoction for so

15

long, we can only imagine what pleasure Alice Payne's sweet brew brought to Segerston's hardworking rustics. They flock't to Alice's cottage, which anon did fill with merry drynkers each night. This, of course, embittered Joan greatly. The woman began defaming Alice Payne to all who would listen—that Alice had Scottish blood on account of her red hair. That she had been born 'neath the malevolent sign of the Scorpion, and practice't heretical sorcery upon her youngest childe, so that forbidden creatures of divination—Demons, mayhap—would appear inside his thumbnail. These slanders caused great tension 'twixt the powerful Deepslough faction, and those others wishing simply to enjoy what scant tyme they had to themselves, with ale that did not taste of unwash't feet...

6

...Anon, this tension spread from tavern to field.

During that summer's ploughing of the Lord Sacrist's fallow field, Ralf Deepslough work't an oxen team with his three burly sons. Nearby, Henry Payne and his grown lad did likewise. As it had all summer, the rain battered down, turning the weedy acres to quagmire. When the Payne and Deepslough ploughs pass't within hailing distance, injurious words were spoken.

Thy wyf be a usurper, cried Ralf.

Alice does not want Joan's crown, Henry replied.

Then why does that brazen whore brew?

Stow thy tongue, Deepslough.

When thy wyf stows her ale. Joan hath always been brewer in Segerston.

By law? We need the coin, and folk be willing to pay.

During this dialogue, Ralf had closed the distance 'twixt he and Henry. Now they were almost sneck to sneck.

Alice hath a succulent arse, smirk't Ralf, *so if more coin she be aft—*

Henry struck Ralf a blow. Tumbling to the thick muck, the two men wrestled together as Ralf's three sons began beating Christopher. The quarrel attracted an audience of other toiling rustics, one of whom was that year's Reeve, a villein whose task it was to marshal and maintain order amongst those working the Sacrist's lands. But while goode with tallystick and calculation, a robust Reeve he was not. Unable to prise the two men apart physikally, he resorted to puny commands—

—Stop this fooling!—

—As Reeve, I command thee both!—

—Return to thine oxen!...

...Feeble entreaties, all of which were lost in the sheeting rain and the grunts of more powerful men than he. In truth, Henry and Ralf might have killed each other, if not for the Reeve's superior—the Bailiff himself—who was then passing upon his horse.

At that tyme, Segerston's Bailiff was named Peter. He had been installed by thy predecessor, Sacrist, and had o'erseen the village's previous thirty harvests. By all accounts, Peter was a hard man, but fair in his judgments. He knew a decent harvest was impossible when a Lord's villeins were too busy cutting each other's throats to cut his wheat. This knowledge had served him well for many decades, and did so again when he climbed down from his horse to put a stop to the ructions 'twixt the Deepsloughs and Paynes.

Riding whip in hand, Peter threatened both families with fines at the next hallmote should they not cease their tumult.

He bade Ralf and Henry's boys split apart, which they did, and for the two fathers to clasp hands in peace. This they also did, though fewe could ignore the lingering malevolence. Nor how Ralf, nursing a bloody sneck, hiss't words 'neath his breath.

Vengeance I shall take upon thee, Henry Payne...

7

...Certainly, his threat would not hath come to pass had Peter lived. An intelligent man of long service and authority, the Bailiff would hath settled Ralf Deepslough's grievance afore he made goode on his promise't revenge. But alas, Sacrist, as you shall recall, auld Peter died not a month later, and was buried in the village church beside the Paschal Sepulchre—a great honour befitting his decades of tireless duty.

Peter's death could not hath come at a worse tyme for the village. The reap was upon them, a reap already teetering upon catastrophe, for the ceaseless rains had rotted much of the crop to slop. Some folk may think it understandable that, face't with ruin, the unfree villeins chose first to save their own crops, and forsook their duty to reap the Lord Sacrist's demesne— *I* do not think it, friends, not *me*—thought I *do* pity that poor, ill-starred Reeve. This same weak man who had failed to stop Henry Payne and Ralf Deepslough battling, now had to remind Segerston's entire villein population of their ancient obligation, and so drive them onto the Sacrist's land each morn afore their own. As ye all might guess, this task was beyond the Reeve. Everywhere he look't, he saw flagrant disregard of custom, and a collective fear took hold that he was powerless to quell. For in each outhouse were the same empty grain barrels and drooping sacks, and all rustics saw in them the bleakest future. Ruination's black fist tightening around their guts...

...their souls...

...squeezing...

...Until, finally, their worst fears were realised and the harvest failed. As the poor Reeve read out the year's Reap Roll, dread filled all who listened. For their stores already wax't scant, and what had been reap't would barely see them through the year.

And there was more disquiet for the Paynes when, during the final day of September, the hallmote jury—weighed down with the man's kith and kyn—elected Ralf Deepslough to the position of the coming year's Reeve...

8

...Friends, how would ye feel with your enemy as your master? To ye guildsmen—all men of urban refinement—the question be alien. But the Paynes were villeins, which be a cruder breed. Thus, they dreaded the viciousness Ralf might unleash upon them. What evil would he enact? And when? Alas, it did not take long for a situation to present itself...

...It was as Pearl had suggested to the youngest Payne boy the night of the bonefyre.

One night a villein—some say his name was Muckle—fled with his family, taking with them all they could carry. But we be more concerned with what they left behind—some forty acres of land and one hundred days labour obligation to work the Lord Sacrist's demesne.

The question was, who would work it?

The law was clear. Blood should shoulder the burden, with either the next of kyn, brother or cousin being compelled to swear fealty to the Lord—to thee, Sacrist—and take o'er land and labour. But Muckle's entire family had fled. He had no known relatives about, so a session of the hallmote court was held in the parish church to decide what ought be done. A juror by the name of Denis Daunt—a Segerston elder of long standing—rap't his fist upon the head table to quiet the gathered villagers.

The coward Muckle hath abandoned his acres and obligations, but also the upkeep of his rented cottage and attendant outbuildings. By decree of the Lord Sacrist, all land, property, and demesne responsibilities must be taken o'er by a villein here this day.

A nervous hubbub amid the villagers. When it died away, Denis continued.

First, be there any person present who wish claim it?

Silence in the church.

Then we jurors vote on who shall take it.

As they deliberated, Segerston's rustics fix't their eyes upon the stone floor, whispering prayers to God they would not be chosen. Though it was not Our Heavenly Father who brought an end to things, but the new Reeve. Ralf Deepslough spoke up to say who he thought should take Muckle's burden.

I vote for Henry Payne, said Ralf.

Seconded, said Denis Daunt.

Relieved to have been spared, Segerston's villeins moved away from Henry Payne, until he stood isolated with his wyf and bairns. Shaking, Henry gathered his voice.

We cannot manage! cried he.

You wish shirk thine villein duties? ask't Ralf. *Put them onto thine neighbours? Fie!*

I seek only fairness, replied Henry.

To the remaining jurors, Ralf said, *Ye be all in agreement?*

Aye, said the jurors in unison.

To the Clerk, Ralf said, *You hast witness the jurors' decision?*

Aye, said the Clerk

Turning to his fellow villeins, Henry said, *Will nobody share this load?*

All avoided his eye as Ralf instructed the Clerk to mark the court roll.

The vote carries, said he. *Henry Payne receives the additional forty acres, plus the attendant one hundred days labour obligation upon the Lord Sacrist's demesne. Come hither, Henry—grasp the rod and swear fealty...*

His wyf and children looking on, Henry hid his face in his swollen red hands. The Clerk reach't for his quill, and with the inking of that parchment, Ralf secured his revenge...

9

...Again, friends, I see the question upon many faces. Why did nobody of true authority—someone not of mongrel rustic blood—put a stop to this abuse of power? *Where was the new Bailiff?* Well, that be a further strand of this tale. Sacrist,

Segerston was thy manor. After Peter the Bailiff died, do you recall who you chose as replacement...?

...Correct, Sacrist! Thomas Harpour of the City of Durham...

...Friends, learning of Peter's death, it was Thomas' father, the Master Mercer Duncan Harpour, who ask't the Sacrist to install his son as Sergerston's new Bailiff. As ye all must know, Duncan was then the Sacrist's personal Mercer. This be the most prestigious position a Mercer in this city can hold, for it be his task to supply the exquisite vestments—the tapestries, robes, brocades—with which the Sacrist adorns this very cathedral and the clergy dwelling therein.

Yet none of Duncan's three sons had followed in his trade. His second-born was himself a Monk at Durham, while the youngest resided in London, reading Common Law at Gray's Inn. Monk and Man of Law—high stations both, bringing great esteem to the Harpour name...so it must hath pained Duncan mightily to witness Thomas, his eldest and heir, stumble from disaster to dissolution.

Thus, Sacrist, though you no doubt had misgivings about placing such a troubled soul into such a vital role, you heard Duncan Harpour's pleadings and engaged Thomas as Segerston's new Bailiff. And who in this room could hath done elsewise? Who here would begrudge a father's plea for his own blood? Thus, as Thomas Harpour moved into Segerston's manor house, he was granted a final opportunity to reverse the wayward course of his lyf...

...Friends, what I would give to end my tale on this dull note. How dearly I wish tell ye that Thomas threw his animus into rectifying Segerston's boggy, blighted fields; the strained alliances 'twixt villagers, and so hauled that place back from the brink. How I wish say that the horror of his tenure did not unleash an undead pestilence upon the land—a rotted monster burning with vengeance and destruction. Aye, I would like to tell that story very much.

But I cannot.

For I be a fabulator of tales, not lies.

Henry Payne found this to his cost during that hallmote, when Thomas did not appear to curtail Ralf Deepslough's revenge upon him. In dede, nobody in the village saw much of the Bailiff at first. He remained in the manor house, the windows shuttered against the day. But the villein servants in that house soon began noising stories of Thomas' strangeness. Whispers concerned his distressing visage, ravaged, some said, by pox. Or worse—leprosy. That he shunned girls and women wherever possible, a truth proven when he turned out from the manor all servants of the fairer sex, and replace't them with his own gender. Barrel after barrel of wine was delivered from Durham, with one scullery lad telling those gathered at Alice Payne's tavern how the new Bailiff quaff't prodigious amounts each night, filling the house with howls of anguish and much smashing of furniture

Thus, in the absence of the canny estate management required of a Bailiff whose manor had just endured a calamitous reap, the situation in Segerston festered further. The threat of starvation loomed, and rustics turned to drynke. Alice Payne continued to brew her superior ale, as Joan continued her evil rumours. And just as the rot had spread through acres of crop, so a similar pestilence crept into the village, turning neighbour against neighbour right as hard winter drew near, and kynship was never more needed...

11

...Fie! My head! It squeezes like a Carpenter's brace...

...I cry pardon, friends, but these skull-bound tempests have plagued me my whole lyf. My only recourse be my medicine, here, in this little leather flask—my soothing syrup. Allow me to take a draught...

...*Ach!* The taste! How I wish it were the wines from the cathedral cellars, for when I was down there earlier, Sacrist, I could not help but marvel at the rare vintages. Prithee, friends, ye should all imbibe! And do not fret o'er me, for my head begins to cease itspaining.

So, where were we?

Aye, hard winter in Segerston...

...Well, winter for a rustic represents respite of sorts. Scant days of thin, glassy light. The fanged wind, whipping across frozen sod, compels them to remain indoors. It be a tyme for threshing and storing grain, though, as I say, there was significantly less of *that* in Segerston that year. Winter also be the tyme for repairs to baskets and pails, for the mending of tools, clothes, and also hames themselves, lest one be amerce't in the hallmote for a crumbling wall or patchy thatch. What outside work that must be done, ought be done apace—gathering fyrewood from the Lord's trees, bracken for the winter bedding of beasts. Come Martinmas, some of those animals meet the butcher blade, their meat salted or smoke't, the blood made into puddings to be enjoyed with loved ones by the fyre.

Only there was no such lull for the Paynes that winter. The Muckle cottage and outbuildings—empty since their escape—were in disrepair. The hallmote had decreed the Paynes were now responsible for their upkeep, so they spent the frozen months shoring joists and tumbled fences. In doing so, they spent coin on pitch and iron nails they could ill afford. So much work was there, that even Alice and the youngest bairn lent their efforts. And with each nail driven—each rotted board replace't—the Paynes felt as if they were constructing their own gallows. This, they knew, was Ralf Deepslough's intention, just as they knew he was not finish't in his machinations— what further misery was he plotting for them?

Friends, they would learn come January's Plough Monday...

12

...and a banging upon their door. Henry opened it to find the Reeve, wrap't in his thickest tunic.

Ralf, said Henry.

Christmastide be o'er another year, replied Ralf. *Where does the tyme go? I trust thee did enjoy the season?*

What do you want?

Aye, Henry! The merriments be done, and the business of labour recommences! I appreciate thy mettle. Very well—on the morrow, I need thee to plough that portion of the Lord Sacrist's demesne once belonging to the Muckles, and now thine.

Henry Payne spat beyond the threshold of his hame.

Ralf, said he, *this be the first thaw in many weeks.*

Precisely why I need thee on the Lord's land.

But what of my own land?

Ralf pulled his tunic tight about himself.

Henry, this bastard wind nithers mine culls. Will you offer me thy fyre?

The Reeve push't past Henry without waiting for assent. Christopher Payne—just gone eighteen now—stood up in attempted masculinity that brought a snort from thick, meaty Ralf. Alice and the youngest huddled by the fyre, where they were spreading grain ready for malting. The Reeve wink't at the bairn, then address't Alice.

It comes to me that in all the blether 'twixt you and my Joan, I have never sup't thy ale. So I wonder, might I do so now?

Ill tyming, said Alice. *As you can see, we be in the midst of brewing.*

Fie, Ralf said, sticking out his lip. *Be there not even dregs from the last barrel?*

Even if it be bitter?

He smiled. *Oh, I be long accustomed to bitterness.*

Ralf appraised Alice's rump as she leaned into the barrel to scoop a cup from the remaining puddle there. Catching Henry's eye, the Reeve made a squeezing motion akin to testing the firmness of a plum. When Alice pass't the cup to Ralf, he swirled it in the fyrelight.

By the Rood, it still hath a head after all this tyme!

He drank.

Mightily fine ale! What be thy secret, dear Alice?

No secret.

No? What about you, little lad? You see thy mammy at work. What does she do that my Joan does not? Do not be afeard, son, you can tell me.

The bairn cringed behind his mam's kirtle.

Enough, Ralf, said Henry. *The ground hath been frozen to iron for weeks. If it be soft on the morrow, I must make ready mine own acres for sowing. My eldest and I, we cannot spend the daylight ploughing the Lord Sacrist's demesne.*

You can plough thine own acres after thine duties to the Lord be complete.

In the biting darkness of evening?

Other villeins do likewise.

Not thine pals, I wager.

Ralf drank off the rest of his ale and stared into the bottom of the cup.

I dare say, Henry, another Reeve might fly into rage at such insult. But lucky for thee, I be of a rarer cut.

You want me to cry pardon, Ralf? Then I cry pardon. I cry pardon for hitting thee.

Ralf mounted befuddlement upon his countenance. *Henry, you think I come here in malice? In petty grievance? In truth you be a mewling, worthless cunte?*

Christopher step't forward, fists trembling. Ralf shook his head.

Stryke a Reeve, lad, and I shall see a hard example made of thee.

Son, said Henry. *Christopher, sit down.*

When Christopher did, Ralf spoke.

You accuse me of o'erburdening thee with demesne obligation so that—what, Henry?—thine own crops fail? Wrong. I nominated thee for thy strength! You work harder than all others in Segerston. By God's nails, I remember when thine two middle bairns died and—

Speak of them not.

—When they died, you were back in the fields the following morn.

Ralf, speak of mine children not.

I speak of death, Henry! Unrelenting death! For it be thy true enemy, not me. Look around this place. Afore the Pestilence, Segerston was twofold in size. Now it be naught but mouldering cottages, wasted lands, and weeds choking us upon all sides. Henry, without you to shoulder Muckle's burden, those weeds shall choke us tighter still.

By the fyre, Alice held her youngest boy. Christopher glowered at the rushes scattered upon the pack't earth floor. For their sakes, Henry Payne mastered himself afore he responded to the Reeve.

Ralf, I say it plain—if I do not begin ploughing my land anon, all shall be lost. Mine crops cannot fail again. I...I must...

Henry's words failed. His whole body trembled. The Reeve sighed.

Henry, you move me greatly, he replied. *And as Reeve, it be within my power to help.*

How? ask't Henry.

Fifteen shillings and you need not turn out upon the Lord's demesne until next month's harrowing.

Henry search't the Reeve's face for sign of a jape, but it was all twisting shadow.

Fifteen shillings, Ralf?

28

Or one of thine oxen.

Why taunt me thus?

Ralf look't sadly upon him. *Be you so hard against poverty's borders? Very well, I have a final idea. I shall cancel thine obligations in exchange for...nay...you shall laugh when I tell thee...*

Speak, man.

Ralf toss't his empty cup to Alice.

The secret to thy brew, he said.

As I telt thee, said Alice, *there be none.*

Cold wind whip't the fyre when Ralf opened the door to leave. At the threshold, he turned.

My father was Reeve, said Ralf. *As was his father afore him, and his afore him. I will not be the first Deepslough to fail a reap. Keep vexing me, and I shall see ye all in rags. Or—*

—Leave this place, said Henry.

Or I shall see thee and thy lad ploughing the Lord's acres on the morn. Which be it?

Ralf, leave.

So Ralf left...

13

...Friends, it will be little shock to learn that, come next morn—the first thawed morn in many weeks—Henry and Christopher Payne were out driving their two-oxen plough upon the Lord Sacrist's acres, and not their own. This they continued in the following weeks, whenever the ground softened. For what choice had they? Henry could ill afford to be fined by the hallmote because the feast of Saint Cuthbert lay a fewe scant months off. Though a sacred day of piety in

Durham—Cuthbert's Shrine be at this very cathedral—for villeins, it also marks payment of rent on their cottages, and land rent for their acres. Henry would be force't to sell part of his dwindling grain reserves to make up the shortfall, and though the previous year's feeble harvest had driven up prices everywhere—especially so with grain—this did not mean his would sell for a pretty sum. Not in Durham. For prices were strictly controlled by the chur—*Mother, fie!* You lumbering clod! Look at me, assuming to explain the convolutions of capital and commerce to a room of the land's most successful Mercers! Urban men who import magnificent silks, cottons, and linens from across the world—weaving in the process great networks of influence from London to Pisa, Andalucía to the Levant. Next, friends, I shall instruct a dog upon the subject of fleas! As a mere Gleeman, I must focus upon the tale. Upon Segerston in the months leading up to the murderous Fell Wraith—her brok arms swinging 'neath the moon—and how she near destroyed it...

...In that year—January into February 1397—the acres were still half-frozen and half-ploughed, the crops not yet sown. Then the feast of Saint Matthius sent winter into retreat and all of Segerston into the fields. The furloughs of the Lord Sacrist's demesne were scattered higgle and piggle amid other private holdings, so that all work't side by side—freemen and villein—at differing purposes, their ploughs like great lumbering needles stitching the soil.

Of course, that freemen rustics work't for their own purses, and villeins for their Lord's, did aggrieve certain bonded folk. But such grutchings were not new. The differing status of villein and freeman was aulder than any any one man born into either category. It was truth immutable, like reaching 'twixt one's legs to find either prick or cunte. Thus, it escape't thinking on.

Though, friends, I do not wish give false impression of Segerston. It was not a place of unseeing ignorance, of continual toil and strife. Despite the hardships, the failed harvest, and the tensions 'twixt some folk, Segerston still found tyme for merriment. There were gatherings and songs, laughter and japing. Betrothals, births, baptisms. Friendships long fostered in the fields by men and women who sweated together as their ancestors had sweated afore them, using the same tools pass't down the generations. Such co-operation also extended beyond the apparatus of plough and harrow, and into the next lyf. The names of all Segerston's dead were inscribed upon the parish Bede-Roll, and when Father Bell read them aloud after Mass each Sunday, the villagers repeated the names of the deceased for to reduce their sentences in Purgatory.

Like all of ye here, I fret o'er the agonies awaiting me in that intermediary place. How many years shall mine bones be shattered there? Mine eyes gouged and mine prevy parts torn by hot pincers 'til I be allowed to join God in his Kingdom? Ten years? A hundred? Ten thousand? This anguish, of course, be ultimate reward for my faith—for I avoid Hell, where the tortures never end—but still, I be afeard. So what comfort, then—what *boon*—for the numbered dead to have an entire community of the living to intercede upon their behalf; to remember their names in prayer so they might endure fewer years in Purgatorial torment. In dede, be there aught more important in this lyf? I think not. For though a community shall always have disputes, the immortal soul binds it together in a far grander sense. A collaboration not only 'twixt generations, but lyf and death itself.

Aye, tis a beauteous thing, but a saddening one also. For as a travelling Gleeman eternally upon the roads, I have no such community behind me. When I die, who will remember my wayward soul? Once, I had my friend, the Gleeman Pearl Eye, but he hath been dead these past six years. Now I have no friend to turn to in my deepest despair, as Henry Payne turned to his closest friend during the final days of February, 1397. His friend, the freeman Adelbert Attwell...

14

...At the head table, Walter Attwell jounces at mention of his father! Do not look so angered, Walter! You be now the Sacrist's own Master Mercer, and hast been since the death of Duncan Harpour. Thy famous name be known far and wide as the greatest Mercer in these lands, thus it be common knowledge thy origin be humble, thy father a simple rustic freeman. In dede, it makes thine achievements all the grander beca—hush, friends! Your exalted peer Walter be trying to speak!...

...Aye, Walter, I hear thee...

...I see...

...Walter, I do not come here to defame thine parents. My own folk—God rest them—raised me better than that. But I *have* been waged to tell the story of the Fell Wraith, that gory, walking ghost. And sadly, thine parents Adelbert and Mabel Attwell be part of the telling, for they were also victims of the Wraith. You would hast still been a boy then, and from what I gather, you were absent from Segerston much of the tyme—boarding at the grammar school in this very cathedral. And when the Wraith brought death upon Segerston, you were already apprentice't to Duncan Harpour in Durham. Walter, be that true...?

...Aye, as I thought. So, Walter, by thy own admission, you were absent before, during, and after what happened. Does it *rankle* thee not to know? To have to pick through the gossips and hearsay like the rest of us? Mayhap you hast heard the ugly whispers about thy fathe—

...Easy, Walter! Again, I be not here for slander! From thy reaction, I see you know the rumours of which I speak. Well, what if my tale snuffs out that tattle for goode? With thy permission, I wish try...

...

...A lengthy pause, Walter, speaks of a mind, split. But I thank thee for thy consent. And now, friends, back to the tale...

15

...So, thy father Adelberth Attwell and Henry Payne were friends. Their cottages lay close by and their youngest boys capered together—the little Payne lad soon to die by the Wraith's hand, and you, Walter. At least, the two of ye would play together when you returned from boarding at the grammar school where you spent much of the year.

Thy schooling was no doubt a great expense to thy father, for though a freeman, he was, in many other ways, not so different to the villein Henry Payne. Both held chattels of comparable amount, and similar sized acreages in which they bent their backs to feed their families. Together, they felt the sting of rising prices and the endless fretting as to what would become of them should the harvest fail again. Mayhap this was why Henry felt his friend would understand if he ask't him for a small money loan...

...Henry saw Adelbert in one of the open fields, driving his oxen plough through an Attwell furlough lying hard upon the border of a furlough belonging to the Lord Sacrist, where Henry was then working. The two men were not alone. Adelbert had with him one of his cottars—that wretched class of men who, while freemen, nevertheless own no land or property, and were thus compelled to live day-by-day in labours for others. Henry was joined by his eldest son Christopher, and his youngest boy, who was just then bringing out to them bowls of meagre pottage and maslin bread. Though Henry Payne pulled Adelbert some distance away to converse in private, the wind blew their voices back to his children.

Adelbert, said Henry, *my Saint Cuthbert's Day rent be light. Would you lend me the difference 'til I can repay thee?*

Adelbert seemed ill at ease. *Henry, mine crops failed as badly as thine own last year, and I have the same unending purchases to make—all dear as peppercorns.*

Henry glance't o'er to where Adelbert's man stood by the oxen plough.

But what of thine cottars? The rents they pay thee?

What cottars, Henry? I have only a handful, and have increase't their rents as much as I can. For what goode does it do if they cannot pay? Adam o'er there, he be in arrears, so pays in labour, but I do not own enough land so that all might do likewise.

A chill wind blew scrim across the hundred-acre field. Henry raised a hand in hail to Adam the cottar, who returned the gesture uncertainly. In years past, Adelbert's firstborn—thy aulder brother, Walter—he would hath been the one standing there, but, of course, sickness had taken him, as it had Henry's two middle children. This was another bond the two men shared, and why Adelbert said carefully these next words—

Henry, I also need every coin for another reason. The new Bailiff, Thomas Harpour, did you know he be the son of Duncan Harpour?

Duncan Harpour? I know him not.

Truly?

Truly, Adelbert. These days, my mind be fastened wholly upon my family's survival.

Duncan Harpour be a famous man, the Lord Sacrist's personal Mercer. At the cathedral, hast you seen the magnificent tapestries upon the walls? The Bishop's glittering robes? The altar brocades threaded with pure gold? Well, every stitch comes from Duncan Harpour.

I have never been inside the cathedral, said Henry.

Of course, said Adelbert, abash't. *I spoke only to explain the following incident.*

Incident?

Some nights ago, Thomas' Valet came to my door to say his Master wish't see my Walter forthwith at the manor house. By God's grace, the lad was hame from the grammar school so, fain befuddled, off we went anon.

Since his arrival, said Henry, *this Bailiff hath rarely been seen. What be thy impression of the man?*

Adelbert shuddered, though mayhap it was only the cold wind.

There be a hardness to him, Adelbert replied. *Yet something else below I cannot form to words. His complexion be fearsome—pox for certain, as my sister Edith lived with such scarring, yet nowhere as severe. And though it was not yet Evensong, he was already long in drynke.*

What did he speak of?

At the start, naught, said Adelbert. *Just mutterings. Then he said his father Duncan Harpour would anon require an apprentice Mercer, and that he—Thomas—had heard my boy was educated at the grammar school. I said that was true, so Thomas made Walter shew the quickness of his mind by repeating his letters and his Latin, arithmetic, astrology—all things, Henry, that be mystery to the likes of us. When Walter finish't, Thomas said the lad had the makings of a Mercer. But if he was to recommend him to his father Duncan, there would be a fee.*

A fee? ask't Henry. *What size fee?*

He bade us leave him without a figure. Only later did I hear talk among other freemen that their lads had also been brought afore the Bailiff.

So fattest purse wins the prize.

Which be why I cannot spare the coin, Henry. For freemen with larger holdings have more at their disposal.

Henry look't to the far horizon, to Newcastle, as if he sought there the words he had next to say.

Adelbert, said he, *I speak the following not to gain thy purse, but to temper thy hope. Would it be such a tragedy if Walter did not become this Mercer Duncan's apprentice? He would still inherit thy freedom. A goodly lyf he would lead, with a goodly fyre to sit afore. That be no poor prize.*

Adelbert waited 'til his friend had spoken his piece.

Henry, shew me thine hands.

Befuddled, Henry did so, and Adelbert the same. All four hands in the same sorry state—the blebbed and crack't extremities of those who had laboured long years in loam.

What be thy meaning, Adelbert?

Adelbert look't to Henry's boys, Christopher and the youngest still watching them.

If Walter becomes a Mercer, his hands will never be as ours. Nor his back twisted. You do not wish that for thy own flesh and blood?

Adelbert reddened then, for he realised his error. In speaking of his own son, he had forgotten the inalterable distinction 'twixt he and Henry—that his friend was villein and unfree, meaning so were his boys. Thus, unlike you, Walter, who spent months away from Segerston while receiving a fine schooling, Henry's lads were forbidden any situation which took them from the Lord's land. This included employment, education...and apprenticeship.

Henry, I cry pardon.

But why? replied Henry. *All you say be truth...*

16

...Walter, members of the Mercer guild—I know Thomas the Bailiff taking bribes to offer entrance to your guild be an affront to your profession. And not only that—offering entrance to *rustics*. Though, it be true Walter does come from such common stock, friends, bristle not! Only a *churl* would dare come afore ye all here to vomit such slander. Everybody knows that thee, Walter—Mercers—ye all possess no peasant traits yourselves, and all earned your place at this feast by dint of canny minds, hard graft, and ingenuity. In dede, what clod could *possibly* equate the work of some shite-shovelling rustic with the important role done by all of ye, gathered Mercers? Ye who sail the oceans in search of the finest fabrics to decorate the finest buildings and finest people? This be your collective purpose and destiny as granted by God. Walter Attwell—God destined thee for the head table this night, beside the Sacrist and his Cellarer, for God hath seen inside thy heart, and shall give thee only what thee deserves, just as God takes from those who do not deserve. This be how *he* made the world. The fault, then, lies in us, in his subjects, whose corruption causes us to see his perfect design imperfectly.

Nor be I exempt, friends.

I, too, learned this lesson in harsh circumstance...

17

...It was one chill season some years back, when Pearl Eye still lived. He and I had been attempting to reach Otterburne, and the manor of a certain Northumberland noble. This Lord expected us by Evensong on the Eve of Christmastide, which we planned to achieve by leaving the employ of another Lord that same morning, whose manor at Rothbury was a day's

walk away. The name of this accursed Rothbury Lord shall
not trespass upon mine lips, save to say we had been entertainment for his eldest son's betrothal, and on the morn we were
due to leave, he had still not paid us for our service. His Clerk
telt us the Lord was away upon some business, though for how
long he would not say. When the Clerk left, I turned to Pearl.

I have heard rumour this Lord likes to weasel from his debts.

Then what do you propose, Mother?

A disagreement opened then 'twixt Pearl and I. At the risk
of breaking our engagement with the Otterburne Lord, should
we tarry at Rothbury to claim what was rightfully ours? Or
leave our current employer without payment, so our tymely
arrival at Otterburne was certain? We had performed for the
Otterburne Lord in the past, so knew he did not suffer tardiness. He would turn us from his doors if we were late. In
such talk, did the two of us clash.

We must stay here 'til he pays, said I.

Nay, said Pearl, *we stryke out for Otterburne.*

And allow ourselves to be swindled?

*Trying to get paid for both risks payment for none. My way guar-
antees one purse.*

Leave here with naught, I parried, *and this Lord shall think he
hath our measure. What then stops him noising about to his peers
that we be soft-touch Gleemen easily cheated? Mark me, Pearl, capit-
ulating today hurts us double the morrow.*

I recall Pearl kneading his knuckles, swollen from the cold
and the years of psaltery playing. From the years in general.

This be rare, said he. *Rare in dede.*

Cease thy riddling. What be rare?

Rare, came his reply, *to find so cloddish a Gleeman.*

Afore I could ask what he meant by that, our decision was

made for us by a number of Rothbury Men-at-Arms who, at the poyntes of their longswords, escorted us penniless to the boundary of their Lord's estate.

It was now as Pearl had said—we had lost a portion of the day without reward from Rothbury, while putting into jeopardy our standing at Otterburne. The weather was wretched rain mired the road. When night fell, lacerating cold rattled our teeth and shrivelled our culls to apple seeds.

Look yonder, said Pearl. *A manor!*

But it was not the one belonging to the Otterburne Lord. This was a ruined shell bereft of roof and many walls. Mayhap it had fallen victim to that rapacious Scotsman James Douglas who, near the end of King Edward's long reign, had so pillaged Northumberland. Still, we took refuge amid the tumbled walls of the place, which, without a warming fyre, were as cold and wet within as without. I fretted we might freeze, so with numb fingers, I fish't a penny from my purse. Laying it upon a portion of fallen masonry, I raised a rock in mine blue fists, preparing to stryke it.

Mother, growled Pearl. *What be you about?*

Bending my penny.

Fie! We shall need that. Help me search this place!

My coin still straight, I did as commanded. With icicled heart, I search't the cellars and that was where I found it—a miracle born not from curved copper, but solid wood. In a collapse't nook, half-buried by masonry and so hidden from ransackers, was a chest made from the richest oak, carved intricately all about. And etch't upon the lid, a name and insignia...

...Dyxover...

...Sacrist, surely you know this renowned Newcastle family of Master Carpenters? Dyxovers have provided chests and armoires to this cathedral for a century or more. Their exquisite containers store the very vestments—the albs, chausbles, cassocks, mantles—procured for thee by Walter Attwell, sat beside thee now. The list of Dyxover clients be long and exalted, lending their work tremendous value. Though there was naught inside the chest Pearl and I recovered from the ruins, it was large enough to house two dozen cloaks and worth more than a villein might earn in a decade. So mayhap you understand my shock when Pearl himself raised a rock above his head, meaning to smite the thing to gobbets.

Pearl! cried I, *What be YOU about?*

Smashing this fukkit chest, what does it look like?

You wish shatter our sole annuity against retirement?

Mother, said he, *if we do not burn it anon, we expire, not retire.*

And he brought down the rock again and again until that beautiful chest was naught but splinter and spelk. As it burned, he huddled close to the fragrant, buttery flames. I did likewise.

Warm, Mother?

Aye, said I, though churlishly.

Pearl sighed. *Shall I tell thee thy problem?*

Prithee do.

You dwell o'er much in the future.

Be that so wrong?

Staring into the fyre that had once been a priceless Dyxover, Pearl said, *For some folk, no. But for the likes of us, futures must be razed to salvage any sort of present...*

...Forgive this digression. For some reason, standing afore ye all this night, I find my dear, departed friend much on my mind. Yet my aside also serves as illustration, for Pearl's words upon poverty describe the predicament facing the Payne family as we return to them in early March, 1397. They, too, knew what it meant to live day-by-day. Henry and Christopher Payne had little choice but to labour for the Lord Sacrist during daylight, and for themselves in darkness, using up their scant reserves to survive just that little longer. As for Alice Payne, she did her best to hysband their livestock, keep their hame and, most importantly, brew ale. This last proved vital, because as the Payne troubles grew, that ale was a welcome source of coin. Though many villagers held allegiance to the Deepsloughs, a goodly number still weighed Joan's accusations of Alice's unnaturalness—her flirtations with thumbnail sorcery—and sided with the woman's superior drop. In dede, many of Ralf's closest allies crept to Alice's door, carrying off a bottle or two to enjoy in secret.

Now the Payne cottage rang with laughter and gossip, but also song. For in a wonderful turn, Alice's youngest bairn—who help't brew the ale but fled to a shadowy corner as the village consumed it—drew closer to the heat of communion until one night, he opened his gob and began to sing. What came out stunned the drynkers into silence, as it had likewise stunned Pearl Eye afore that damp bonefyre. Such a honeyed voice none had ever heard, and from then on, his voice—his confidence— grew. A wight came with an auld tambour to beat out a pattern for the lad to sing to, filling the Payne hame with jigging villagers. His own mother, too, who swayed her hips merrily.

As for Henry, despite the grief it caused with the Deepsloughs, he took great pryde in Alice's ale being the best in Segerston. He was also pleased his youngest lad—whom he secretly fretted was o'ersoft—seemed to be coming into his own skin. But above all, Henry Payne was relieved by the additional coin. Even with the brewing fees owed to the manor, it cushioned the blow of the increase't tyme he was force't to spend upon the Sacrist's demesne, meaning he would be able to purchase at least *some* of the provisions he had not tyme to grow himself. He even laid hands upon a second fermenting barrel, so that Alice might increase production. By his calculation, if they could find a third barrel—then a fourth—and begin selling the delicious brew at market, they just might survive the year...

...Which, of course, be when Fate's wheel takes a grim turn. I cannot vouch for the exact truth of what happened next. Like toss't straws, many versions lie oblique to each other, though I once heard the following sang by a Gleeman in Monkseaton—

> *They drank the ale for the ale was slick,*
> *And sat by the hearth for the hearth was warm.*
> *Then sickened anon for they had been trick't,*
> *As she cackled anon for her plan had been born...*

...Again, friends, I cry pardon for the rustic composition. But forgive its crudeness and ask yourselves—who be this *she* so sung of? Who concocted the evil plan? Upon first hearing,

43

why, naturally ye assume Alice Payne. Or mayhap that corrupt, worm-chewed Wraith who even now be said to traipse 'neath the moon. Yet, step slantways, friends, and appraise the thing from a different vantage—does not another explanation shew itself? Allow me to breathe lyf into this alternate premise...

19

...Imagine, friends, we be scant days from the start of Holy Week, that most sacred tyme when Christ was crucified and born again. Alice had gone into the fields with pottage for Henry and Christopher, leaving the bairn at hame, spreading grain for malting. But no sooner had she gone away, than a shadow fell across the doorway.

Bonny lad, said Joan Deepslough, *Be thy mammy about?*

Timid without his mother, the boy said naught.

Fie, said Joan. *I wish speak with her upon a matter of importance. Might she be long?*

I know not. Mayhap.

Joan seemed pleased with this answer.

Aye, you be a canny lambkin. How auld be you now?

Ten, said the boy.

So young! Yet I hear thy voice be fain powerful. Would you sing for me?

The boy look't at his feet.

Ah, shy lad. But, lo! What be that by the fyre there?

As her hysband Ralf had done, Joan entered the house without the boy's permission. She saw the spread grains, the second ale barrel in the corner.

A-bubble for Holy Week?

Joan took the lad's silence as invitation to continue.

Remember Father Bell's lesson after Mass last Sunday? When he spoke of the seven grievous sins, especially that of pryde? Well, lambkin, his words pained me, for I have been proud o'er thy mam's ale. I would not admit its superiority.

From the malting pan, Joan pluck't up a sprouted grain.

It be a mystery how something so small can be naught in the hands of one, yet transcendent in another's. What makes the difference? Love? I cannot tell thee how much love I give my brew...yet it does not shew in the taste. So if not love, lad, what?

To his horror, he realised Joan wish't his opinion. But she spared him by flicking the sprout into the flames, where it burn't away.

Lad, I believe it something innate. An additional wit God grants some folk. Pryde stop't me from accepting God's will, but now I wish cry thy mam's pardon for my conduct towards her. For the wrong things I have noised about. There be sufficient strife in Segerston without also quarrelling with thine neighbours, do you not agree?

Stricken, the boy look't to the empty doorway.

I wonder, said Joan, *might I take a tipple of her ale while I wait?*

Joan went to the second barrel, lifted the wooden top. A heady aroma escape't.

Smell that! How fortunate only meat be forbidden us during Lenten, and not ale. For who can afford meat, anywise? Be there a cup I might dip, lad? Run and fetch one.

Like most rustics, the Paynes kept their eating and drynking things inside a wooden box in the loft. The lad clambered up the ladder, found a cup, returned anon. Joan dip't it into the ale and drank. Her smile was like the string of a longbow, nock't.

It be everything they said, and more! Though it needs more days' maturing, it be already greater than aught I have brewed. And you help't make this?

Aye, said the boy.

Joan shook her head in wonder, handing back her cup.

Wash it and return it to its place.

He did as was telt. In the outhouse water barrel, he rinse't and dried the cup, then place't it alongside its kyn up in the loft. When he was done, Joan was stirring the ale with the long paddle used for that purpose.

The foam built o'er large, so I brok it up.

She hung the paddle back upon the wall, smiling widely.

I shall take me leave, so you can finish malting. Best I return later and speak to thy mam then. Do not tell her I was here, nor about supping her ale. At least, not until I cry her pardon, for until she forgives me, it might be to her eyes yet one more stolen liberty—and thee will be punish't for allowing it. Understand, lad?

Aye, said the boy.

Joan smiled wider still.

Bonny lad, said she. *A bonny, canny lad and no mistake...*

20

...Friends, what tainting substance Joan deposited into the barrel while the lad cleaned the cup, I cannot say. Dried foxglove, mayhap, which those troubled by block't constitutions know induces a purging of the guts. We can only judge by the effect, which shewed itself the following Holy Week, on Goode Friday...

...The Payne family entered the church,

watch't by the sickened faces of those who had drunk Alice's ale the previous night. Their sweating visages further agonised as they crept and crawled on hands and knees to kiss the Cross, ashamed of their befouling stench and trumpeting backsides as they lit candles afore the Paschal Sepulchre. This last was drape't in rich vestment, friends—a cloth no doubt made by some long-dead member of your Mercer guild. Deep vermillion it was, embroidered with scenes of Passion and Resurrection, of Tortures and Hellmouths disgorging Devils, Imps, and Wraiths. And in each groaning belly, every rancid fart and spew, there sounded the accusation that the Paynes deserved to be roasted by those very fiends for all eternity.

Leaving church that day, those healthy folk who had not sup't Alice's ale help't their poisoned neighbours hame. Joan Deepslough, who of course had not drunk the Payne brew, had leaning upon her arm the shuffling figure of the villein woman Matilda Lodes. It was to Lodes that Alice spoke.

Matilda, you hast drunk gallons of my ale with no ill effect.

Matila groaned against Joan's shoulder, leaving Deepslough to reply.

A cunning ruse, said Joan. *To poison more, first gain their trust. Matilda, listen to her not! I did not do this!*

Mayhap that be true, said Joan. *Mayhap it was not you.*

She peered behind Alice to where her little lad hid.

Leave him be, said Alice, shaking.

Many in the village be saying it, said Joan. *After all, he takes after thee in looks, so why not in malice? The two of ye brewed that noxious concoction in tandem.*

My boy did naught I did not tell him.

Ah, so you admit thy conspiracy! Did ye hear? Did ye all hear her words?

47

Joan address't the remaining congregation still loitering in the churchyard, all of whom look't fain ill. All with hard eyes upon Alice Payne as Joan continued her accusations.

Was it the Devils in thy childe's thumbnail that bade thee poison thine neighbours? Or simple envy that we Godly villeins can bear our burdens whilst ye, feckless Paynes, cannot?

Matilda, said Alice weakly. *I beg thee, prithee believe me.*

When Alice reach't out to touch her shoulder, Matilda's eyes sprang wide. Misery wrought upon her pallid face, she unleash't a torrent of spew down herself. With a final groan, she fainted into Joan.

Matilda, I—

Stow thy tongue, witch! said Joan. *Hast you not done enough...?*

And they moved off with the rest of Segerston, leaving the Paynes behind...

21

...Yet wise auld Father Bell was long-attuned to unrest amid his rustics. He knew the shape of their grievances, and so waited in church on Holy Saturday for Henry Payne to finish lighting a tallow candle at the Sepulchre—one stub feeble in weight and material, its trembling yellow light outshone by the sturdy wax offerings of those with greater means. Father Bell watch't Henry bow his head in prayer for all the dead Paynes—Father Bell knew their names, had baptised and buried many of them—and when the villein turned to leave, the Priest step't from the shadows.

Might we speak, Henry? Mayhap in the churchyard?

Henry agreed, for he also wish't talk with the Priest upon

a serious matter. It was something Henry should hath done months ago, though each tyme he bent his step to the Priest's door, he had lost his culls and turned back. He hope't it would not again be the case.

They went into the churchyard. The cold, lichen-mottled wall surrounding it was dark with the years and elements. But it was sturdy in contrast to the haphazard portion running south from the church, bulging a half-acre outwards afore joining the original, much aulder construction. Built of jagged and uneven stone, the new wall was already beginning to slip— the work of unskilled men in great hurry—and though it was afore the tyme of most, all in Segerston knew the expanded churchyard dated from the Great Pestilence. Folk had been dying so rapidly, in such hideous manner and number, there had been nowhere left on consecrated ground to bury them. In desperation, the empty lands beyond had been bless't, and a new wall thrown around them, allowing those still living to keep pace with the mountainous dead.

There were no markers, the bodies had been lowered into great pits. But Henry knew somewhere 'neath his feet lay tumbled an uncle, two grandparents, a sister, his mother and father. He himself had been barely a year auld, raised up by a cousin the hallmote had commanded take on his father's lands and demesne obligations until he, Henry, came of age. Such arrangements were common in the shattered months and years following the Plague. In dede, even some fifty years later, the population had not recovered and landowners still struggled. Where once a Lord had always been assured of plenteous villeins to work his demesne acres to profit, now the opposite was true. Lords would therefore not grant freedom from bondage to their remaining villeins, but for the heaviest purse.

Thus, Henry found himself victim of past and present combined. He was twenty years aulder than either of his parents had ever been, a notion which never failed to send him reeling. And now he had to do something which made mockery of that seniority. To the Priest, Henry said his long-practise't words.

Father Bell, he said. *My family be in need of alms this Easter Day.*

The Priest's frown rattled him, for it was an expression he had not anticipated.

Henry, said Father Bell, *when I am by a man's deathbed, fighting the Devils that wish pluck away his departing soul, I cannot be soft. I must interrogate the dying man harshly, for if I do not provoke him to full confession—do not bring afore his eyes all his guilt in the scant tyme left to him—then he shall be lost forever. Thus, I do not muzzle mine next words to thee.*

Henry could only nod as Father Bell continued.

Henry, many of the congregation have been sickened so greatly they could not come to church in worship of Christ during his most Holy Week. And they say thy wyf is to blame.

Nay, Father. That be base lies noised about and no more.

But that is not all, Henry. I also hear thee struck the Reeve? And quarrelled publicly with the hallmote jurors when they gave to thee the villein Muckle's demesne obligations?

Unfair obligations, Father. Ralf Deepslough leverages his station against me in fulfilment of private grievance.

Darkness was falling; a heavy sky belaboured with cloud. But Father Bell's eyes shone hard, excoriating light.

You admit no blame? Not for thy wyf or thyself? Henry, this is the sin of pryde.

Not pryde, Father. Truth.

The Priest snorted in derision.

You speak of truth? Well, here it is—you are villein, and villeins abide by ancient custom. They work the Lord Sacrist's demesne without complaint, for God hath made it so. By creating such discord 'twixt thy neighbours, you refuse him and threaten the very survival of this place. That is the truth, Henry! For to threaten the Lord Sacrist's harvest is to threaten Segerston itself.

To have such words directed at him—from no less a figure than Father Bell—Henry felt the very blood fall from his veins. Trembling, he look't about at the mortal remains of those who had lived and died in Segerston across more years than he could imagine. Father Bell cleared his throat, and Henry brace't himself for another barrage of scorn. But the Priest did something strange. Reaching into the wide sleeve of his surplice, Father Bell removed what Henry first thought was a stalk of wheat. Only it was the wrong tyme of year for that crop, meaning he had kept it a goodly span for this purpose, whatever it might be. The Priest held the stalk up to the diminishing light, so they could both see better.

Simple wheat, aye? ask't Father Bell.

Warily, Henry look't at the Priest, who smiled.

Henry, I do not test thee. Is this or is this not wheat?

Not, Father.

Then what do I hold?

Darnel, Father. False wheat.

Father Bell twisted the stalk 'twixt his fingers. *But it appears the same?*

Aye, said Henry, growing more animated now they were speaking the language of fieldwork, the language he knew best. *But look, Father—darnel grains be a touch longer in comparison, the ear less whiskered. Tis true they look apiece, but to a learned eye th—*

Henry reddened at his presumption to tutor the likes of Father Bell.

Henry, wheat and darnel grow shoulder to shoulder—or ear to ear—do they not?

Aye, said Henry, *to the disadvantage of the wheat.*

For we cannot eat darnel.

Aye, Father.

Yet darnel appears the same as wheat, or almost so? And grows amid it?

It does, Father, said Henry, growing wary once more.

The darnel stalk vanish't into Father Bell's sleeve as sharply as it had appeared.

Henry, our talk puts me in mind of Matthew's Parable of the Wheat and the Tares. You know this word, tares?

Tares, Father?

An ancient name for darnel. False wheat. Lolium is another, which is why we name those fiendish false Priests Lollards. You are no friend of the Lollards, I hope? For their heretical teachings shall see God smite thee.

Nay, I know no Lollards.

That heartens me. Well, in Matthew's Parable, Christ speaks of a field in which some enemy had maliciously sown the evil seed of tares amid the wheat. These tares grew apace, and in alarm, the Reaper ran to his Master to ask permission to pull up those weeds and burn them. That is what you do with darnel also, is it not Henry?

Aye, father.

But the Master's crop was not yet full grown, making it fain dif-ficult for the Reaper to know which plant was goode and which bad. Thus, the Master denied his Reaper, lest he waste his true wheat alongside the false. Quoth the Master: "Let both grow together until the harvest and in the tyme of harvest I will say to the Reapers, Gather ye together first the tares, and bind them in bundles to burn them, but gather the wheat into my barn." Henry, do you comprehend?

Father Bell saw the fast-flowing panic 'neath the surface of the villein's face.

Henry, if the wheat is Mankind and reaping Final Judgment, then what is the barn?

Henry opened his gob to speak. Closed it again.

The Kingdom of Heaven, said Father Bell. *That blissful place where only true wheat—those who accept Christ's love and teachings—shall be saved. False tares are men who reject Christ. Disruptors sown into the field by the enemy, and so shall burn in Hell. Henry, who might this enemy be?*

The...Devil, Father?

Aye, said Father Bell in satisfaction. *The Devil. And remember, that fiend sows no matter the season.*

I weed the darnel—the tares—each year, Father. Wherever they appear.

I know, son. But Christ's words carry a deeper meaning. He speaks of spiritual and social discord. One I see growing in Segerston. One I see sprouting from thy family.

Henry almost swooned. Feebly, he replied, *I be a Godly man. I know my Paternoster. "Pater noster, qui es in...in caelis san—"*

Henry—

"sancto...sancTIficetur nomen...nomen tuum—"

I believe thee, Henry.

"Adva...Adveni—"

HENRY, ENOUGH.

Two fat crows heaved up from the ground. Father Bell composed himself while they clack't and cawed o'er the church spire. The Priest watch't them fly into the lead sky, and did not look at Henry as he spoke.

There are Priests that deny shrift and housel to those who refuse the order God gives mankind. Some even excommunicate these

*wrongdoers. Henry, it would break my heart if you did that to me.
I beg thee, do not make me do it.*

As you can see, friends, Father Bell loved his congregation
deeply, and did not wish deny them sacrament and absolution. Henry knew he had upset the Priest. Great shame wash't
o'er him, but Father Bell spoke as if he knew the currents of
Henry's mind.

*How many thousands of drifting, famish't souls would give all
to take thy place? Thank God for your position, Henry, for you hast
tenure to land. A wyf and children who love thee. Thus, it is thy duty
to reconcile all things. To live with what God asks of thee.*

Aye, Father.

*Start by crying pardon to Ralf Deepslough. And thy wyf, she must
admit her guilt.*

...Father.

The Priest took a final look around the churchyard. *And if
not, then...*

Then what, Father?

But Father Bell went inside the church to prepare for
Easter Day...

22

...Mercers, mine unceasing travels about the
land usually find me elsewhere than Durham during Holy
Week, so I be curious to learn how your guild celebrates the
sacred day that Christ was risen. Do ye receive sacrament
here at the cathedral? Or in your parish church of St. Nicholas,
which abuts your stone guild house in the market square? I
must say, friends, each tyme I enter St. Nicholas, I sink deeper

'neath its spell. Hundreds of churches have I visited, in hundreds of towns, so I can say with authority that it be one of the finest in the north—nay—all England. Unequalled opulence! That rood screen painted with the richest images, the carved processional Crosses, the silver and pewter candlesticks, chalices, thuribles, and osculatoriums—no equals have they, and that be *afore* we speak of the vestments. Mercers, the *vestments*. The albs and tunicles, copes and surplices—all stunning. The Lenten veil ye possess there, friends, I *wept* when I first saw it.

And I saw, also, ye have built a separate altar within St. Nicholas, partitioned off for sole use by your Mercer guild. And a Priest waged to sing Masses of your own composition and choosing. How fine it must be to dictate the contents of God's succour, so that ye may go about your business becalmed.

But that be your right, Mercers.

For ye pay for it with thine business successes...

...And how God loves you for it...

...As for me, I take what I can get. Unattach't to any trade or religious guild, my name absent from all Bede-Rolls, I attend church in whatever place I find myself. Since coming of age, rarely have I confess't to the same Priest twice and, unlike most rustics, I do not wait until Easter to receive shrift and housel. In dede, I seek to be cleansed of sin as often as I be able, for the Gleeman profession—surrounded by gayness, feasting and drynke—does multiply the Purgatorial sentence more rapidly than other trades. Pearl Eye, he used to jape and jangle me after I returned from the shriving pew, the

55

taste of Holy Sacrament still upon my tongue, *Thy Heavenly Soul now wears fresh hose, Mother? Tis a pity thy Bodily Arse does not.*

But I do not wish speak ill of Pearl, only to say my Gleeman friend's verbal lashes shall hurt far less than the ones awaiting me in the next lyf. Aye, the torments of Purgatory clamour my mind just as they did when I was a bairn. Back then, above the chancel arch of our parish church, I recall there was painted a depiction of the Day of Doom. I see it still—rendered by a crude hand. Leagues away, Mercers, from the masterwork gracing your St. Nicholas. Yet the primitive nature of the images mattered not to me. I was *terrified* to look up at Jesus floating in that blackened sky, watching his Angels shepherd those Righteous Ones cleansed of sin into the Kingdom of Heaven, while the world below was torn apart. Fiery rents in the earth spewed forth hideous walking corpses, their grinning faces alive with worms, their rotting arms wrap't tightly about the naked, forsaken sinners left behind.

Aye, that dread frieze be what I remember most of Easter Day as a lad—standing below it during the long wait for my turn to step inside the shriving pew and confess to the Priest. Just as the rustics of Segerston waited that long-ago Easter day, as we return to the tale...

23

...And to the Paynes, shuffling in line across the stone flags of the church. The only sound was the mutter of Paternosters 'neath breaths, for no rustic knew the meaning of that prayer's Latin words—as they likewise did not know the contents of the Masses Father Bell read to them each day—but they *did* know the Priest would ask them to recite the Paternoster as proof of their faith. Thus, like starlings duplicating human voice, they repeated the sounds as best they remembered them. Henry's youngest boy listened to their broken phrases with a leaden heart, not because he feared repetition of the prayer itself, but because he worried about the questions that always came after—

—*Hast you envied thine neighbours?* —

—*Been gladdened when they fell to harm?*—
—*Begat rumour or did not stop others begetting?*—

—*Chafe't against God's Will and his plan for thee?*—

—*And so sown discord...?*

...For he *had* sown discord, had he not? He had let Joan Deepslough into their hame and she had done... something he was unable to understand, but which he knew resulted in the scorn his mother now endured. Mam had made him man of the house that day, and he had failed her. Worse, he had colluded with Joan, for he had never spoken of the woman's visit. After the disaster of Goode Friday, Mam ask't him if aught had happened to the ale—had he made any alteration to the recipe, however innocent? She even whispered her secret words into his thumbnail to beseech it shew what transpired to make the barrel noxious...but the pale disc of his thumb remained blank. The boy had been glad of this, for he was afeared of what Mam would say if she knew. Afeared of what Joan might do if he blabbed.

57

And terrified to tell Father Bell he feared both more than God's wrath.

Would the Priest see all this coiling like coalsmoke about his young heart? Would he forbid him from joining that second line of shriven souls awaiting housel—the Host upon their tongues—and the final cleansing of their sins? And when the Day of Doom came, would he then be hauled, screaming, down into the Pits of eternal Hell? Such questions the boy was fretting upon as he watch't his mammy, first of the family in line, step into the shriving pew...

...And did not come out...

...The Priest's low voice could be heard above Alice's weeping. Eventually, she staggered out in distress and Henry flew to his wyf.

I cry pardon, said Father Bell, emerging from the pew, *but if you refuse to confess thine sins, I cannot shrive thee.*

Sins? said Henry, anger and fear thickening his voice.

She knows full well, came the voice of a villein in line, one who had spent Goode Friday upon a bucket, shitting outwards his inwards.

Henry ignored him. *Father, my wyf be no poisoner. You must shrive her.*

I cannot. Nor can I shrive thee.

Father?

For you did not heed our talk. You did not cry pardon to Ralf Deepslough.

Redoubled by the stone walls, the Priest's words drew the attention of all. Henry's indignation failed him.

There hath...there hath not been tyme.

You speak lies afore the Cross?

Mine boys, said Henry. *At least shrive mine boys. Forgive their sins.*

Tears sprang to the Priest's eyes. *I cannot, for they are still under thy governance. Oh, how this stabs my heart!*

In anguish, Father Bell withdrew into his pew, while his Sexton ushered the Paynes out of the line, unshriven. Alice went off weeping, leaning upon Christopher, with the youngest clutching her kirtle. But Henry refused to move. He opened and closed his gob as does a fish pulled from the weir. As if he wish't say something to Father Bell. To his Sexton. To the hundred or more folk staring at him; folk once friends and neighbours who, unlike his family, would soon receive the Sacrament and be cleansed of sin.

But no words issued from Henry, and he left the chur—

24

—Friends, we be interrupted at this tragic moment by yet more food! What do the servants bring in this tyme? Haunches of roast venison! Truly, I be humbled by your capacity, but then, men of your station be difficult to sate.

Sacrist, Cellarer, Walter, and gathered Mercer guild members—while ye devour, perhaps we take leave of our principal tale? For I do not wish taint your food with the Paynes and their misery. In dede, yonder venison puts me in mind of a strangeness that befell Pearl and I many years gone; a tale involving a dreadful creature that hath doubtlessly birth't as many songs and as much drunken tavern blether in its place of origin as the Fell Wraith does in Durham. In dede, I see many

parallels 'twixt the two, so mayhap telling of this other frightful monster shall enhance our understanding of the Wraith. So
what say ye, friends? Would ye like to hear? I swear, this story
be as juicy as the flesh ye all now chew...

                                                    ...Your lusty

cheers say aye!...

                              ...Well, it happened only two or three
years after Pearl Eye had taken me on as his apprentice. I was
still a sprout, hairs barely upon mine culls, and hard upon
learning the Gleeman trade. Our seasonal gyration—by which
I mean Pearl's gyration—rarely moved further south than York,
a place with which all here be familiar, there being a guild of
Mercers in that city with which ye conduct much business. In
the shadow of the minster there—which I must say does not
approach the majesty of this cathedral—we were playing in the
street, when a man came and introduce't himself as an Agent
of a certain Lord. Said the Agent, his Lord's son was to be wed
one week hence, to the daughter of a Lord of equal stock. The
perpetuation of two glorious lineages remains the vertebra of
our great England, and it was this Agent's job to secure entertainment for the bless't event. The estate was a goodly portion
more south than our usual route, in a lonely place some days
walk, but the purse was too fat to refuse.

The next week, following the Agent's scant directions, we
became lost. Pearl thought we must continue east along the
road, while I believed turning north, through the woodland,
was the better course. We bickered, which was when God sent
to us a wayfaring rustic with a fardel of straws upon his back.
To this fellow we ask't who was correct 'twixt myself and

Pearl—road or woods? The wayfarer telt us the Lord's manor lay beyond the woods, but became frantic when I bent my step in that direction.

Nay! cried he. *If you value thy lyf, stay on the road 'til it bends north. Though doing so shall add burdensome miles, it be better than never arriving at all.*

Why? ask't I. *What lurks within? Wolves? Bandits?*

The wayfarer cross't himself. *Would it were either such workaday horror.*

Then what? beseech't Pearl.

But the wayfarer had already said o'er much. He spat upon the ground and continued on his way, casting nervous looks to the treeline as if the evil he had spoken of there lurk't, poised to spring.

The rustic's fear caused us to circumvent the woods. After all, we were professional Gleemen with a contract to fulfil, and would not risk tardiness through entanglement with some mysterious arboreal entity. We thus arrived to the manor tired, but intact. The Lord himself greeted us warmly, treating us as his guests and not waged entertainment. This he did for the others under his employ, all of whom hailed him as the most generous man in the land. Our quarters were warm and spacious, the food the richest I have eaten—especially the venison, which to this day be the tenderest ever to pass mine lips. In dede, this Lord was famous for his venison, and had made himself doubly wealthy from its sale. He raised the deer in the very woods the wayfarer had warned us from entering.

Aye, a rare tyme it was. For the next three days, we entertained those gathered for the betrothal. Pearl and I were but two of a troupe of Gleemen, Bards, Shawm-Blowers, and

Mummers dressed in fabulous disguise. During lulls in the merrymaking, we ask't these more local artisans if they had heard aught strange about the venison forests nearby. It was clear by their expressions that they knew of what we spoke, but did not wish bring evil upon themselves. Yet one stern soul—a Saltatrix, if memory serves—let slip that, in a cave in the heart of that place, there dwelled a horrifying creature. A thing which walk't upon two legs, but was twice the size of a man, and covered all about with thick, reeking hairs. A thing with wilde, glowing eyes as sharp as the teeth it used to rip open any wight foolish enough to enter its domain.

Gleemen, said the Saltatrix, *I speak of a Woodwose...*

25

...Friends, as Mercers, many of ye have travelled to every corner of England and beyond—across oceans to foreign climes in the procurement of fabrics. Ye be all well-journeyed men of experience, so mayhap ye have heard speak of the Woodwose. The Saltatrix gave description of this brutal thing's appearance, but allow me to recount its character. Woodwoses be Nature's most bestial creation. Purest distillations of violence and cruelty, they course with an insatiable lust for women to ravage and bairns to chew upon. Among rustic populations, the Woodwose be greatly feared. In dede, many a mammy uses its legend to terrify their bairns into staying out of the trees, lest they be made a meal of...

...As my own mammy did me...

...Aye, well. Mayhap this was why, when Pearl declared his intention to seek out this particular Woodwose, I was terror-struck. After the marriage of the Lord's son was done, I pleaded with him to return north, but he refused. Early in our acquaintance, Pearl and I often found ourselves at odds in this way, though, lo, now I say it, that never much changed. But I was still a boy then—so young I now appear as a dream to myself—and was thus unable to counter the man. And mayhap it was not only my lack of years that hampered my attempt to declare myself. I suppose, too, I was still mired in grief, for I had lost my family in cruel fashion and was alone in the world. That stark truth numbed my soul as ice press't to flesh renders it insensible.

In those first years of our acquaintance, I received scant succour from Pearl in this regard. The man kept his distance. At the tyme, I thought he considered me a burden—for when in ale he would say thus—but later, when I gained the capacity for reflection, I saw differently. Like me, Pearl had lost his own family. His mother had died when he was an infant, but his father, Gervase, had been a Gleeman of great rank, retained at Appleby Castle by the fifth Baron of Westmorland. There, he had played for other noble families, and Plantagenet Royalty such as Edward of Langley. It was expected Pearl would follow in his father's step and be to the future sixth Baron what Gervase was to the fifth. In dede, the lad was already shewing great talent in this regard, but then another Gleeman took up residence at the castle. This famous man had once been part of the third King Edward's court and delighted the Baron's guests with tales of royal intrigue. Gervase could not compete, and anon found himself relegated to supporting player. This blow was great and, like innumerable souls afore and since, he fell into bitterness and drynke. Eventually, the quality of Gervase's playing so declined that he and his son were expelled from the castle without letter of recommendation, as they were soon cast out from a slew of further houses of diminishing rank, 'til he found himself playing taverns and common greens, drynking away what coin he earned from both.

In drunken fury, Gervase began to beat his boy regularly, taking from his childe what little joy remained to him, and also half his sight when a smash't shard from an ale bottle thrown by the father pierce't the boy's left eye. This violence mark't the beginning of the boy's transformation into the Gleeman known as Pearl Eye, a name he used evermore in place of the one he had been given.

Pearl had been no aulder than ten or eleven years when all this befell him—no aulder than I was then. Thus, mayhap I reminded him of his own pain, and far from lacking compassion, Pearl was giving me tyme to collect the scattered kernels of myself. To gather the pieces the way auld folk glean reap fields for wayward grains...

26

...And so we return to the morning after the betrothal of the Venison Lord's son, with Pearl Eye and my own self—young Mother Naked—venturing into his woods in search of the Woodwose.

The low sky churned. Trees crowded dankly, groaning and swaying in hymnal, their bloody trunks smeared with shed antler velvet. I wish't not to be there, but Pearl was the only person I knew in the world, so I followed him deeper into the forest. Transfix't, he barely notice't the brambles tearing his tunic and flesh, until eventually we crested the top of a heugh. Peering down into to the valley below, Pearl whispered—

A cave!

Yet it appeared to me more as a hole directly into the Pits of Hell, for, remember, I had seen the Day of Doom painted upon the chancel arch of my own parish church. Above the heugh, a tambour of pain beat in my skull, but I saw none of the flowers we call Devils-bit from which to make a soothing poultice. Pearl was already creeping down the slope, to a boulder granting cover. I went in his wake because the only thing more frightening than nearing the Woodwose's lair was being left alone. Then, once behind the rock, we waited...

...And waited...

...And waited 'til the sky grew so dim we risk't being in the trees come nightfall, and not even Pearl's ravenous curiosity would allow that. But when we began to take our leave, a figure approach't the cave.

The Woodwose...

...Friends, sometymes when repeating tales, the particulars become inflated. Some wight in a fight, when retelling the story to his mates o'er ale, may double the number of foes he fought. And in this manner, you might expect the Woodwose described by that Saltatrix to hath been similarly augmented. But nay. If aught, she had been *conservative* in her portraiture, for the thing afore us was truly monstrous in appearance and proportion, covered head to foot in matted fur, and so tall it had to duck its shaggy head to enter the cave. Anon, thick grunts came from within. The chink of flint, the glow of fyre.

Grinning, Pearl grip't my wrist.

We go closer, he whispered.

Pearl, I beg thee.

Think on the tale you shall one day tell of this, said he.

I care not for the tale.

Neither shall thy audience if it ends here, pissing thyself behind a rock. Come.

Thrashing would make noise to alert the Woodwose to our presence, so I let Pearl pull me to the mouth of the cave. A powerful stench came from within. Peering around the lip, I saw no sign of the creature, only a modest fyre and the scattered bones of creatures consumed. These remains horrified me, for I could not be sure if they were animal or human, but then Pearl grip't my head to direct my sight upwards to the cave's ceiling.

And I forgot to breathe.

By fyrelight, I saw how it was carved all o'er with the most perplexing, interlocking patternwork—akin to curling hart-tongue ferns was my first thought—which spread across the ceiling of the cave and down its walls. Looking at the ferns flowing and entwining, my sore head quietened. I felt myself being pulled upwards like regress to the womb, suck't back into God's mind. And I was on the verge of this oblivion when, from the deepest part of the cave, the Woodwose step't out. The towering fiend filled the place, feverish eyes aglow. It opened its huge, gob and...

...And, friends, I remember naught, for

I fled; my animus reduce't to pounding blood and twin lungs bursting for the faltering daylight beyond the treeline. There, I collapse't in a heap. When Pearl emerged from the forest a hundred yards away, my fear he had been eaten alchemised to rage. I beat at his breast, furious at the danger he had put us in.

I thought I was to be eaten!

God's nails! said Pearl. *My first notion was the stories WERE true!*

He exhaled a long and trembling laugh.

You laugh? And what means "first notion?"

You were o'er-busy shitting thyself to see his "hair"?

His hair?

Woven rushes, sewn higgle and piggle with animal furs and his own hairy flesh.

I had not seen so. Terror had expunged my mind.

And when he opened his gob, his tongue was missing. Cut out.

What of it?

That was no Woodwose, said Pearl. *That was a man.*

A man? Then what happened to him? Oh, Pearl, why did you take us there!

For thy education, said Pearl. *I must take on thy father's role, now he be gone.*

You be not him! Never would he teach such a lesson! What do I learn from that?

As intended, mine words wounded him. Pearl's face darkened and I thought he might clout me, but instead he lowered his face to mine. Hot plumes of his breath gusting.

The lesson, said he, *be this—we tell tales of what lurks out in the dark so that we need not acknowledge the truth within.*

What truth?

That, oftentymes, the fiend be our fault. Do you understand?

I thought of the Woodwose-man's cave, the intricate wonder he had carved therein. I though, too, of other things. My own past.

Aye, I said. *I think so.*

Pearl look't as if he did not believe this.

And hadst you been wrong?...HAD it been a monster?

He pinch't my arm.

Then you be a stringy cut of meat, so Sir Woodwose would be flying to the privy...

...Friends, I speak of this tale because th—

27

—Cry pardon, friend? Speak loud, goode Mercer, for mine ears be as auld as the rest of me...

...I see...

...You ask the Woodwose man's fate? Aye, a noble question, and one shewing thy compassion, for even in the throes of merriment, you find it in thyself to worry o'er the less fortunate. You be of fine character, sir, a quality which no doubt vouchsafes thy seat at this Mercer feast!

Well, friends, it so happens the genesis of that poor creature I *did* learn, though at a much later date. They be origins of much tragedy and strangeness, but I shall reveal them anon, when they will make greater sense. Now, we ought return to

Segerston, in the year the Wraith spread disaster, and to the Paynes in particular. Though, I suppose, the outcast Woodwose lends handy comparison to the status of the Payne family then, for both were pariahs in their separate ways. The Woodwose in his venison forest; the Paynes in Segerston—their infamy complete after Holy Week by dint of being the only unshriven souls in the village. And so, they languish't in mistrust, exile, an—*Fie!* My head again makes merry!...

...I cry pardon, sir, what did you say...?

...Nay, kind Mercer, I shall not partake of the wine. Believe me when I say it would not help, and besides, I would not deny thee of a single drop. Instead, I take another pull at my syrup bottle...

...Ah...

...Now, where was I...?

28

...Aye, the hallmote following Holy Week. Alice was amerce't a hefty sum for the production of noxious ale, and forbidden ever making more. This was easily done, for after her devilry had been noised about, no wight within fifty miles would drynke it.

Joan Deepslough's brew once again became *de facto*, and she

regained her position as the quivering spyder in the gossamer
of Segerston salacity. Under the thatch of her hame, inflamed
by her unappealing yet untainted ale, were nightly discussions
concerning the Paynes and the troubles they had caused. Many
had become ill from her Holy Week brew and fallen behind not
only in working their own land but also, if they were villein,
in their demesne obligations to the Lord Sacrist. The inherited
status of their bonded blood compelled them first to redress
the balance to him—to thee, Sacrist—afore they might recoup
losses on their own land.

And it was upon the land where these grievances found
the Paynes. Spiteful words directed at Henry and Christopher
as they ploughed and sowed. Not only that, as March gave
way to April, Ralf Deepslough, in his capacity as Reeve, continued heaping upon Henry the most laborious ploughing and
digging of the Lord's land. In desperation, Henry attempted
to use his dwindling monies to wage cottars to work his own
holdings while he and Christopher were abroad the Sacrist's
demesne, but there were scant cottars willing to work for
the unshriven hysband of a known poisoner. And those who
would, still did not. They were compelled to find better-waged
work elsewhere, for their freeman landlords had increase't
their rents to compete for the Mercer apprenticeship offered by
Thomas the Bailiff.

Thus, having no friends remaining—even Adelbert Attwell
was busy with his own problems—and not able to pay for the
help he needed, Henry brought his wyf and youngest into
the fields. If we close our eyes, friends, mayhap we can see
them across the gulf of forty years. Four thin figures upon the
demesne afore the sun hath even risen—Henry and Christopher
at the oxen-plough; Alice driving their stubborn dray horse to

harrow o'er the seeds afore the crows found them, seeds of oats and vetches sown by the dibbling stick of the youngest boy...

...Thus far, I have spoken little of this lad. In the many tales and songs of the Fell Wraith I have heard, this boy, if he appears at all, does so only when perishing inside the burning manor house. His feeble scattering of years cast into the flames—

> *Burn't Benches, burn't Bailiff,*
> *Burn't Beams and the Bairn,*
> *Burn't the Doors, burn't the Floors,*
> *Burn't the whole of that Hame.*
> *Burn't Table, burn't Ladle,*
> *Burn't Thatch and burn't Latch,*
> *The saved become Dust,*
> *The damned naught but Ash...*

...To die painfully and unshriven, 'tis a sorry end for any, but doubly so for one as young as he. So let us breathe *lyf* into this boy and bring him to the centre of our stage, afore the years roll o'er and he be forgotten forever. As we all shall be in tyme.

He was a timid boy. A shy lad who, when singing for his mam's patrons, had for one moment begun to bloom. But when Alice's ale came to an end, he retreated into the shadows once more. His only friend, a man who now sits foremost amongst you—Walter Attwell—was at that tyme away for long spells at the grammar school, and the rough capers of the other Segerston lads frightened him. After the events of Holy Week, those boys made him the target of their scorn.

One day, when Henry and Christopher were labouring

71

upon the Lord Sacrist's demesne, and Alice tending their own lands, the hame work was left to him. Young Payne went to forage deadwood along the fringe of the Sacrist's woods, when the three Deepslough brothers Philip, Theobald, and Bertram came upon him. Flashing a knife, Philip threatened to cut off the boy's be-Devilled left thumb—the one Alice whispered her spells into. Terrified, the young Payne boy ran, but the Deepslough brothers were bigger and the chase did not last half as long as the beating that followed.

Afterwards, mewling and snivelling, the lad stumbled to the stone wall circling the acres of the Bishop's deer park. Against the mottled stone, he fell to weeping. Wept until his stomach ache't. Wept until he heard steps approaching...

...You, Walter, coming through the trees. You, Walter, bowing deeply to reveal thy gleaming, tonsured skull.

Castratus, you said.

Henry's youngest dried his eyes.

Canum pediconem, he replied.

Ita vero, you said. *Semper idem.*

Friends, I be gladdened to hear laughter and not disdain from those of ye who speak that tongue. These were young lads, after all, to whom crude insult be warmest affection. The reason Henry's youngest—a simple villein who had never seen the inside of a school room—could speak tolerable Latin, and also knew his letters, arithmetic and logic, was because of thee, Walter. Whenever you returned hame, you taught to him that which you hadst learn't. And though thy rustic friend was denied education by dint of his villein status, he was neverthe-less equal to thine lessons, absorbing them fully and practicing

them during the long spans you were gone from Segerston.
A Segerston which you saw, Walter, had been much altered.

What is this malaise about? you ask't. *Many folk now scowl so.
Do you see it?*

I do.

And what of our fathers?

Our fathers, Walter?

Yesterday, at the well, you said. *My da hurried from thy own
without speaking.*

The Payne lad shook his head. All he could tell his friend
was that Ralf Deepslough was tormenting their lives. At
mention of the Reeve, Walter, you made a *porcinus* face.

The Deepsloughs, you said. *Suckling piggies down to the last!*

Both lads laugh't, and it felt goode. Like it had once been.

At school, you said, *we are served sucklings for Saint Barnabas.
Capons and trout, too, and mutton with goode wheat bread.*

Walter, ask't the Payne boy, *hast you ever eaten darnel?*

*Prick-fondler, are you simple? You cannot eat darnel! But no
matter, hear this—I do not return to school for a fortnight, so we can
pal together.*

Henry's youngest said he would like that very much, but
then Adelbert—thy father, Walter—came out of the trees.

Son, said he to thee, *come away. Supper awaits.*

Father, might we both come?

Walter, come away and do not speak back at me.

So you went with thy da. Walter, you did not see, but
Adelbert look't back o'er his shoulder at the Payne boy as if
the lad was some meddler upon foul business. And for those
weeks afore you returned to the Monks, the only tymes ye both
saw each other was while working in the fields, across the span
of many tilled acres...

29

...Walter, you look troubled. Do you feel well...?

...Aye, Walter...

...Aye, you ask a valid question. How *would* I know of this encounter? At school, thy logic was exceptional, thus the answer ought not tax thee...

...Correct. *I be Henry Paynes' youngest.* I did not perish in the burning manor house. Instead, I—

...More fevered talk at the head table! Though it be too low for mine ears, I understand it still. Friends, while it be *true* I was once a villein bound to Segerston by blood, it hath been longer than one year and one day—much longer—since I departed.

Which means I be free by law.

I have committed no crime except the omission of who I be, which be no crime at all. For how many among ye here this night conceal certain parts of yourselves? I was merely trying to draw ye all into the Fell Wraith's tale—that foul and evil ghost—by unveiling its mystery in proper sequence, for greatest effect. That be my training as a Gleeman, and I can no more ignore my training than a Potter might purposely throw a haphazard jug. And I be not finish't unveiling the Wraith. Friends, should I continue...?

...Sacrist, hear thine pleading
guests! They wish me go on with the tale...

...But *still* the
head table be unsettled! Walter, I address thee directly. Aye,
for my minor deception you *could* raise the Constable to cast
me into the slymiest cell in North Gate gaol, but do so, and
you shall never know what causes thy father to laugh so.

Aye, Walter, I thought that detail might snare thy wits! I
know thy da Adelbert still lives. More than eighty years auld he
be, and residing in Gilesgate, in the Kepier Hospital there. You
never visit him, do you? But I do. Each tyme I pass this way, I
go in secret. So I know of the madness that struck him dumb,
and how from that day to this, Adelbert hath never spoken a
word of what happened that night. Or in dede any word at all,
for he spends his days in laughter, does he not? Laughing for
nigh-on forty years, moon-struck by the terrors he witness't
when the Fell Wraith brough murder to Segerston.

For this reason, he hath never telt of how his Mabel—thy
dear mammy—died. By all accounts, her death that night was
not a goode death, was it? Her corpse found slash't apart as if
by some creature not of this world. Does it not *gnaw* upon thy
mind, Walter, to know her fate be tied in some fashion to that
Wraith? That only thy father knows for sure, and his mind be
estranged from his tongue? Walter, believe me, I know the pain
of being on the other side of the wall to those you love, which
be why I come to help thee climb thy own. To speak that which
thy father cannot, and so bring thee peace...

...And Sacrist,
dear Sacrist—what of thee? Since tyme out of mind, Segerston

belonged to the Sacrist of Durham, yet in one night of blaze and blood, this Wraith turned thy village into a mass grave, one to rival any dug during the Great Pestilence. To this *day*, nobody knows what occurred. Sacrist, you be a man of natural curiosity—do you not crave the truth of what happened to thy God-granted property? Well, this night, I offer the final pages of that book.

Grant me leave to read them for thee...?

...Thank thee, Sacrist. And thank thee, Walter. Now I shall continue the tale by returning us to the young Payne boy, who be now my auld self...

30

...After my beating by the Deepslough brothers, I scarcely dared go abroad alone. I believe this was why, seeing my misery, Da took me for the first tyme to Durham market, so that I might escape mine troubles, if only for a fewe hours.

Friends, most of ye in this feasting hall have lived in Durham your entire lives, which might be both blessing and curse. Mayhap this place hath become stale to you as week-auld crust? If so, to each man here, when the storm now blowing outside finally abates and my tale be done, I bid thee go out and view this marvel of a city with new eyes.

And in doing so, become me as a childe.

Think on what stirred in my breast as I approach't the city walls that first tyme. For though I lived scant miles away, I had never seen the place. Segerston was situated upon a long heugh partway up the north side of a longer rise, obstructing all views to the south-lying city. Village lads dared each other climb the summit—as they goaded each other to leap the wall of the Bishop's deer park abutting Segerston—but I was o'er meek to do so. But now, with my father carrying a fardel of precious grains upon his back, we crested the rise together and set down the slope towards Durham. Friends, I was awed at the sight— the cathedral resplendent upon its stone spur, as high above the city as God be above the Earth. With each step closer, its magnificence loomed o'er all, and I was unable to look away, yet also afeared. How could an edifice of such magnitude be of this world? The sense of scale Segerston had nurtured within me since birth blew apart, causing me to reach for Da's hand.

But alas, my troubled father was unable to soothe me. His journey to Durham was no simple mission of mercy on behalf of his boy—the additional demesne obligations had put further stress upon his plough, bending the iron ploughshare. To engage a Blacksmith required him to sell a portion of his depleted grain reserves. The work would not be cheap, so all depended on him getting a goode price. Thus, my father was pensif of mood as we cross't Framwellgate Bridge and climbed Silver Street towards market.

We reach't it as the Steward opened commerce by pealing the day-bell. An inauspicious sound, for anon did Da find himself arguing with a second Steward o'er the increase't entry-fee, afore bickering with a third regarding the fix't price of the grain itself. Afeared by their violence, I slip't away to find a quiet corner, but the market was in full thresh. Never had I witness't such tumult! Men roared out their wares—butter and beans and bream; timber, tools, tar—their words twanging different to how they were spoken in Segerston. Below their stalls, the bravest rats nip't at fallen produce and were chase't off by stout ratting dogs.

Mine five wits assailed, tears prick't mine eyes. But then I heard a new sound—psaltery music, played sweetly from the edge of market. Pulled towards it like a fish upon a line, I came, Mercers, to your stupendous stone guildhall nestled beside the church of St. Nicholas. A man stood there, strumming his psaltery.

A man with a silver-clouded left eye...

31

...Pearl Eye was a Gleeman unique in performance and philosophy. Unlike Melchior Blanchflower, the man I replace this night, Pearl held no attachment to a court or noble family. Nor did he desire it. The regular stipend, the annuity in retirement which allows aging players to blow upon the final embers of their lives in peace and security, it was not for him. Likewise, did he eschew the refined verse of such Gleemen, for they be as incomprehensible as Latin to the crude rustic, just as the inverse be true of wandering players, whose doggerel smut sounds like mulebray to those highborn. And while it be not so unusual for a travelling Gleeman to be retained a day here or there by a noble house—as Pearl and I were at the betrothal of the Venison Lord's son—their patrons be generally of the lower orders, a truth which shews in the scant weight of their purse. This makes it hard for Gleemen who make their livings upon the roads to save enough coin for their dotage, and leads, o'er tyme, to embitterment. Force't by threat of destitution to traipse from town to town to earn his bread, a Gleeman wishing to hang up his psaltery on the morrow, might come to resent the audience he plays for today.

But not Pearl.

Whenever he slip't away, I could always find him not by bending my step to the most affluent doors, where our peers congregated in the hopes of employment, but by going to some infamous place. A tavern or common green populated by rustics of every stripe—cottars, villeins, freemen, and vagabonds—and there would be Pearl, trembling in the delirium of creation, wringing every last drop of his animus into some song. Mayhap his audience thought him mad. I confess, more than once, I did likewise.

Children especially compelled him. As I myself had done at Segerston during that feast of Saint John, the little ones sought him out wherever they could. Pearl let them. For many years, I was not sure why this was so, for children least of all could wage him. Later, I understood that was the very reason. Thus, when Pearl saw me overwhelmed at market, he strummed his psaltery all the sweeter.

Pearl recognised me as the boy from the bonefyre, and we spoke at length. I sometymes wonder if our conversation that day altered my lyf evermore. Did it doom me or save me? Friends, I still do not know...

32

...See me at Durham market, the skinny scrap of bairn creeping towards Pearl Eye as if he were the Cross at Eastertide. See Pearl strum dreamy-like, his face turned up towards a springtyme sun still ice't o'er with hard winter. He sings so low upon his breath that I must edge closer still. The song was an auld one, and Pearl rarely sang it for other than himself, because it created stronge and unpredictable feelings in audiences. But as Pearl's partner some forty years, I heard it so often it hath sodden my mind the way rain soaks cloth. Taking up my psaltery, I shall play it—

Ask't Fat John to Cottar, "Is there tares in mine wheat fields?"
Said Cottar to Fat John, "Tis true, I suppose."
Ask't Fat John to Cottar, "Why did thee sow them?"
"I did not sow them," said Cottar to Fat John, "Mayhap
ask the wind, wherever she blows."

Mayhap ask the wind, wherever she blows...

Ask't Fat John to Cottar, "Are you shameless or idle?"
Said Cottar to Fat John, "Neither of those."
Ask't Fat John to Cottar, "Then why tares in mine wheat fields?"
"They be one and together," said Cottar to Fat John, "Where
you find the one, so the other shall grow."

Where you find the one, so the other shall grow...

...Pearl turned his goode eye upon me, so I stop't my creeping and became as a statue. Then he shut that goode eye and finish't his song—

Said Fat John to Cottar, "Uproot and toss them."
Said Cottar to Fat John, "That would add to thine woes."
Ask't Fat John to Cottar, "To whom do you speak, churl?"

*"A great man of import," said Cottar to Fat John, "of wisdom
and splendour, as everyone knows."*

Of wisdom and splendour, as everyone knows...

Cried Fat John to Cottar, "Where goes my goode wheat?"
Said Cottar to Fat John, "All pulled from thine rows."
Ask't Fat John to Cottar, "But what shall I now eat?"
*"Or what shall eat thee?" ask't Cottar to Fat John, "Wheat,
tares, and Fat John—fine feast for the crows."*

Wheat, tares, and Fat John—fine feast for the crows!
Fine feast for the crows!...

...By the end
of this ditty, I was at Pearl's feet. The Gleeman let the last chord
fade afore he address't me.

Did you enjoy my song, lambkin?

Ever-timid, I nodded.

That gladdens me. But did its true meaning snare thee?

Tares be bad, said I. *And ought not enter the barn.*

You know this word, tares?

From Da, said I, with some vainglory. *Least, I heard him telling
Mammy about what Father Bell telt him about tares.*

Matthew's Parable, said Pearl. *And what else did Father Bell tell
thy da?*

I churned mine brains 'til the answer came.

That tares be another word for darnel.

A sharp wight, Father Bell, said Pearl. *What do you know of
darnel?*

It cannot be eaten.

81

True! Pearl strummed a bright chord upon his psaltery. *And only what can be eaten can also be sold, aye?*

I reckon so.

Another chord. *True again! Only...look yonder.*

I followed Pearl's decent eye to where it settled upon my father, still quarrelling with the market Steward.

Thy da there, said Pearl, *he fights with an Agent of the Church. It be that other man's task to secure first purchase of his grain, and set the price thy da must sell it.*

Pearl could see I did not understand, so gave a lesson.

Think on it like this, lad—say you wish purchase a bushel of wheat. Do you want to pay a lot or a little?

A little, said I.

Pearl strummed a third gay chord.

So you buy it for a little, use a bit thyself, and wish sell on the rest. What price would you want to sell it? A little or a lot?

A lot.

A fourth chord, higher still in tone.

Well, lad, that be what the Agent wishes do to thy da. For in these modern tymes, we cannot even sell grains we CAN eat—

33

...Friends! I beseech you, hold off judgment of what I say! Quieten thine hisses and boos! Only a base churl would *dare* come into these hallowed chambers to blaspheme so! To spread vile slander such as the Church be naught but sucking leeches! Nay, I repeat Pearl's words because they form part of Segerston's terrible fate, one that be a lesson for us all. If there ever be a tyme to hear how best to live an honest lyf and avoid such an awful end ourselves, surely it be today, upon the feast of Saint Godric. That exalted hermit be Patron Saint of your Mercer guild, a man who lived o'er a century in devout service to our Lord Jesus Christ.

So hush, friends. Allow me to finish recounting Pearl's words, and I shall shew them to be in all ways the reverse of what a man must speak if he wishes, one day, like ye all here this night, to be admitted into God's Kingdom...

34

...And

speak Pearl did, for he had not finish't his lesson.

So, lad, the Church compels thy father to sell them his grain for pennies at market. He might feel aggrieved at that, aye?

Aye, I said, but quiet-like. Young as I was, even then I felt the transgression.

But then, said Pearl. *The solution be plain—why not sell it at markets elsewhere? At Derlyngton or Spennymor?*

When I nodded, Pearl shook his head.

Doing so would see thy da amerce't harshly in court, he said. *As he be amerce't for so many things. Amerce't for grinding his grain upon his own stone, and not the Lord's mill. For baking his loaf in his own oven, and not the Lord's oven. For fishing the Lord's weir and snaring his rabbits. For burning his wood. For plucking his fungus. For entering into labour and leaving it. For marrying, and marrying off bairns. For brewing ale. For tithing and church rood screens and windows of coloured glass. Even fees to pay after death. And if any wight dare question the why of it, the answer be simple—for this be custom and hath ever been thus.*

83

The deluge of words unfooted me. Pearl struck a troubled chord.

All at steepest price for those who can least afford it. And look, there, the result.

At a nearby stall, two rustics argued bitterly about a bushel of grain.

They fight like stoats in a sack o'er prices neither one hath set, until both lack the strength to ponder who did set them.

Stewards pulled the men apart and lead them away up Saddler Street.

Where be they taken? I ask't.

North Gate gaol. And while they suck slops in a dungeon, others eat lean meat with pepper. Tell me, lad, hast you heard speak of a man named Wat Tyler?—

35

...Nay! Jeer not at mention of that man's name! The Sacrist granted me *permission* to tell my tale, so I must do as he enjoins!

Said Pearl, *Hast you heard speak OF A MAN—*

—A

MAN NAMED WAT—

—NAMED WAT

TYLER...?

...Friends, I *assure* you I also shiver at the mention of this infamous fiend. Long did I debate whether to taint the evening with his name. But now I have done so, mayhap the following shall placate.

For I once met a man in Guisborough that some local rustics said had been part of Wat Tyler's rabble during his so-called Peasant Rebellion. This man, they said, had rampaged with Tyler through Kent and London, and was present for the razing of John of Gaunt's palace. Yet, far from some proud warrior-rustic, they poynted out to me a shrivelled auld man deformed by violence. He had escape't Smithfields, so I was telt, where Tyler himself was cut down in 1381, but with then-King Richard's men at his heels, he was force't to abandon his wyf and bairns, and had been on the hoof ever since—a shattered auld wight in the corner of a tavern, annihilating himself with ale.

What a miserable lot for a man! And sure proof, Sacrist, in the Church's teachings. For goode Priests tells us the corporeal head be akin to the ruling classes, and we could no more remove the head and expect the torso to function than could the feet—the supporting peasant masses—be any other place than at the bottom. This be the Divine labour system which the evil rustic Wat Tyler sought to upend, making England as a Saltatrix walking upon her hands—feet in the air and noble crown tumbling from her head into some stinking puddle! Thus, God meted out to Tyler and his followers such brutal punishment. We all know what happened, friends, so if it helps, keep that in mind as we return to Pearl's description of that rebellious man...

36

...Wat Tyler was a rustic like thee, said Pearl Eye to me. *A rustic harried on all sides by laws to keep his wages low, even after the Pestilence had raised the price of his labour. A rustic crush't by poll tax after poll tax upon his person to send yet more armies to fight the French. Rich men found ways not to pay these taxes, so the rustic bore the brunt. Folk already in hock just to exist, for the poor be never more than a groat from the grave.*

At Pearl's words, I look't for Da. The Steward had gone away, leaving my father slump't by a stall.

Lad, said Pearl. *I speak to thee.*

I turned back to the Gleeman.

The rich man treats the rustic as tares even as he commands him cut his wheat. Tell me, does thee recall my song's refrain?

I hesitated, then suck't in a breath and sung aloud.

Wheat, tares, and Fat John—fine feast for the crows!

Pearl jounce't at the beauteous sound.

Such lungs! But aye—Fat John, that's the wight. Well, lad, imagine what might happen if we "tares" decide to no longer swing scythe for bastards like him?

I do not recall my reply. Mayhap my mind was filled with murderous black crows gobbling up Fat John, their bloody beaks deep in his opened guts. Though I do remember Pearl telling me that Wat Tyler and his men had said *nay* to all the Fat Johns of England. *Nay, no more.* And in places further south, they had changed things. Now villeins there lease't land like freeman, without obligation to work their Lord's demesne. Villeins free to go hither and yon as they pleased.

Proof, said Pearl, *the long-held precedent governing our lives be not so immutable after all. And does it not beg another question?*

What question?

Which other iron laws of custom might really be formed of wax? Many rustics of England now be wondering so...though, alas, fewer in the Palatine of Durham.

Pearl jutted his chin up at the cathedral, towering o'er the market.

Say Wat Tyler's name in the shadow of yonder edifice, and you may end up like Master Oink there.

A Butcher was walking in the direction of Fleshewergate, hoisting upon his shoulder the carcass of a headless pig.

Do not look so afeard, lad! said Pearl. *Our talk be not of pork, but darnel. You telt me it could not be eaten, but what if that was not true? That most simply refuse to consume it for they be afeared of what they might see?*

See? You see with thine eyes, not thy belly.

Pearl closed his goode eye, so only the clouded one remained open.

Do I see with this?

This was the first of many thousands of tymes that he would do this jape upon me.

I learn't so, continued Pearl, *from a wise man who owns many books on physiks. The organs all be connected. Thus, the lungs can speak and kidneys hear. Thy heart, too, can see. Darnel makes it so. Folk fear that—seeing what their hearts see.*

Why?

Because oftentymes, it sees what they wish not.

Not knowing how to respond, I ask't the one question I could conceive.

You hast tried it?

Darnel? Aye, on occasion.
What be the taste...and sight?
Pearl played a final chord, discordant and beautiful.
Strange, said Pearl. *Strange both...*

37

...Again, friends—
Sacrist—these be *Pearl's words,* not mine. And though I did love
my friend, I never telt him I think on our meeting that day
with something akin to regret. For I escape't the destruction of
Segerston, where many others did not.

Where my family did not.

So, with his seditious talk of grain prices and Wat Tyler,
had Pearl sown tares into my boyish mind? Tares I then carried
back to Segerston, where they germinated and brought down
the Fell Wraith's destruction as punishment upon the village?

It pains me to think myself the unwitting source of
calamity. That evil seed growing in the loam of my mind.
Matthew's Parable teaches us darnel be indistinguishable from
goodly wheat, and as I lay unsleeping upon my pallet that night
after market, listening to the vermin a-scuttle in the thatch, I
know it was not Wat Tyler's bloody peasant rampage that filled
mine thoughts. Nor any injustice—*imagined* injustice, friends—
committed against villeins by the ruling classes. Nay, the first
shoots of tares appeared as something altogether different.

As Pearl Eye himself.

For there was magic about the Gleeman. His lyf was ungov-
erned by plough and harrow. He was at liberty to wander
where he pleased, which was forbidden us Paynes. Yet the

man's physikal roving was but a tangible fraction of the thing because, though the one-sighted Gleeman did not grow crops, he still created. Pearl's songs grew in the hearts and minds of his audience, and that spoke to something inside me I could not then express even to myself. The delicious low quiver in my belly as I sung for Mam's patrons was a sensation I had not felt again since the end of her brewing. But I had felt it at Durham market that day, listening to Pearl. It was not *what* he had said—sooth to say, except for the part about darnel's queer taste, I understood little—but rather *how he said it*. With a crack-ling animus that turned mine gizzards to darting swallows. Young as I was, might one day I inspire others to feel likewise? Lying awake, I glimpse't the possibility of a lyf other than the one I led, one which caused guilt to swell my breast. For God had made me the feet of the Body Politik, not the head nor any other part. I was villein. To dream of being other than what God chose for me was sin most grievous.

So, friends, I ask you—how much of the coming tragedy be my fault?

Did I sow the tares of Segerston's fate?

Listen, and make up your own minds...

38

...Thus far, Thomas Harpour the Bailiff hath remained obscure in our tale, reflecting his minimal involvement in Segerston affairs. So how best understand the man? Mayhap we might do it by first understanding ourselves.

Friends, would it surprise you to know I be learned upon

the body's inner workings? Well, it be true, and for my knowledge, I be indebted to one noble family residing not far from Durham. Many here shall know the Lamberts of Lumley. While Pearl Eye still lived, it was our custom to perform for the Lamberts each Hocktide. Then, once Pearl met his sad end, I continued doing so alone. In years past, the Lord was one Lancaster Lambert, whose firstborn son Eric suffered from falling sickness. Lancaster search't long for a cure to vanquish the illness that so plagued his boy. He took great interest in physiks, apothecary, and the study of the humours, yet, lamentably, Eric succumbed to his malady in his twelfth year—a tragedy which only redoubled Lancaster's desire to learn all he could about the caprices of the human vessel. He corresponded with the wisest Infirmarers from across the land, from Bristol to Bury St. Edmunds, and amass't a great collection of medical texts by ancient Saracen and Greek scholars—Avicenna, Hippocrates—all transcribed at great cost by the Monks at this very scriptorium.

Though I was a low-rank't Gleeman, and he a noble man highborn, Lancaster and I grew into goode acquaintance for reasons I shall later tell. In his kindness, he allowed me access to these texts, among them treatises upon the intricacies of humoural balance. Its hot yellow bile, and cold, wet phlegm; the black bile and crimson blood that bridge those two extremes. I learned how a man's composition of humours be cast by his birth 'neath one of the twelve signs, as bequeathed by God. For he makes unique dispositions for each one of us and, in doing so, primes us for our given roles in this lyf.

Friends, take myself. Look upon me, a decrepit wreck of almost fifty—stoop't and grizzled and gimp't in the knee from the thousands of hard miles I have walk't about these northern lands. From Alnwick to Westmorland, south as far as York, then east to the Humber—I have entertained at feasts, markets, and betrothals. I have played in the hames of noblemen and gentry. Cooper and cottar. Burgher, Blacksmith, Beggar. Nigh on *forty years* of circling these places and peoples—rich and poor, free and unfree—singing and telling mine tales. For I be a Gleeman! To perform thusly, I must first stoke myself to flame, so that I might ignite similar fyre in my audience. But I was born a low rustic, and rustics be cold creatures of Phglem. As such, this Gleeman heat be not natural or safe to my constitution. I cannot run fiery hot indefinitely, lest I burn up like an acorn toss't into a hearth. I must cool myself 'twixt performances. Victuals help—cold, wet repast of cabbage and herring return mine humours to the chill state into which I was born. Long days spent in mindless toil likewise snuff out my o'er-inflamed mind.

But not ye all, Mercers! Ye three dozen men afore me now—men of commerce, capital, civic duty—your high-rank't souls be of yellow bile. Hot, dry men of great import; urban men who live in stone houses within the city walls. This natural heat transfers to your profession; the power *radiating* from the exquisite vestments with which the Sacrist drapes this cathedral, its Bishop and clergy. Mercers, in this way ye make Durham the greatest city in all the world. Yet, only through continually stoking your heat might ye achieve such monumental feats. Ye must consume hot venison and boar, red wine, mead. Peppercorns from the Ganges and cinnamon from Cathay, shook from the wings of monstrous, flame-breathing birds. Why, take the magnificent feast ye have just eaten—at my foot lies a scorch't peacock feather—which your innards be now transforming into action and genius...

...Mercers,

this be why ye all blaze so bright in this world...

...Yet

Lancaster Lambert's books also warned of another category of man—queer anomalies that defy science by refusing their place within God's natural order. Do we not see them abound in these troubled, modern tymes? Treacherous men who bring down Doom upon themselves, and anyone in their shadow?

Well, friends, Thomas Harpour was one such clammy case...

39

...One which filled Segerston with rumours of his queer behaviour and frightful appearance, and yet more so after the freeman George Goodsell returned from Durham, bringing with him further information about their new Bailiff. In Joan Deepslough's tavern, George telt his mates of speaking with a disgruntled Councillor. This man, said George, had been in some low den for common men—not unheard-of for those of rank to enjoy the occasional roughness—and was fain cockeyed with ale. To George, he grutch't that Thomas Harpour owed him a fat purse from dice. Nor, said the Councillor, was it the only purse the man owed about town.

But then, said George to his mates, then the Councillor jape't, "Harpour ought be a better gambler, for he wasted not his youth chasing cunte!"

The Councillor telt him that when the Bailiff had been a lad afflicted with pox, his condition was so grave a Priest was called to provide for his imminent death. This Priest shrived

him by hearing his whispered confession, then gave housel—
the Host place't upon his tongue to swallow—thus allowing
him to die a goode death.

Yet afterwards, said George, *young Thomas lived.*

His mates cross't themselves, as I see many here do now. To
be curse't never again to lie with a woman, or eat meat? Aye,
friends, to *survive* being given final rites and thus denied those
pleasures evermore, mayhap that be a worse fate than death.
One to drive a man to madness.

And how far be madness from depravity...?

40

...Though
Henry had never step't foot in Joan Deepslough's tavern, he
nevertheless knew of these whispers about Thomas, and
they clamoured his mind as he approach't the manor. For
weeks now, Ralf had continued heaping demesne work upon
Henry. Then, in the midst of this toil, another villein, similarly
o'er-burdened, absconded from Segerston, taking all he and his
family could carry. And it was because he knew Ralf would
seek to burden him with this absent villein's demesne obligations, that Henry did the unthinkable and went to speak with
the Bailiff himself.

He knock't upon the back door and the Valet opened it.

Certain songs give this Valet's name as Osbert, for he, too,
lost his lyf to the Fell Wraith. Osbert was not of the village, but
had come with the Bailiff from Durham, presumably because
he was accustomed to his Master's queer ways. I cannot say
whether the nature of his employment had soured the man, or

if he had been born thus. Either way, Osbert look't down his sneck at Henry as he enquired what the villein was about.

Replied Henry, *I wish speak with the Bailiff upon an urgent matter.*

Does Master expect thee?

Nay.

Then speak to the Reeve, who shall speak to Master.

The Reeve be what I wish speak on.

Osbert flash't brown teeth.

Look at thee, said he. *Smeared all about with shite, and expecting audience?*

The open door afforded Henry a view inside the manor. By now, most of Thomas' servant boys had fled his employ, leaving chaos unbound—upended furniture and dark spillages upon the stone floor. At the sight, Henry struggled to gather his culls and address Osbert.

Prithee, sir, this be in thy Master's interest also.

And how might the likes of you know what be in Master's inter—

The Valet was interrupted by a crash deep within the house, then a loose and terrible scream. When it died away, Henry and Osbert look't at each other. For a moment, the villein glimpse't something other than the Valet's contempt.

Fear.

Then all was as it had been.

Master cannot see thee, said Osbert, shutting the door...

41

...So, Henry did not see Thomas until the man's appearance at the following hallmote, where the Bailiff was joined by another man. Friends, it be tyme to bring into our tale the final member of the head table. The silver-haired fellow now sitting at the Sacrist's right hand—his former Cellarer, Hugh de Tanfield. Now, Hugh, you be in thy *ninth decade,* and look at thee! Truly, you seem as hale as you did forty years gone, when you attended that Segerston hallmote of April 1397. As Cellarer, it was thy duty to o'ersee all seven of the Lord Sacrist's estates, ensuring each Bailiff managed his particular manor well, and all proceeds from their demesne harvests reach't the Sacrist's purse unmolested. In this capacity, word of the precarious situation in Segerston must hath reach't thine ears, compelling thee to come in person and assess the state of things.

Do you recall that day, Hugh? It was a lyfetyme ago, and you surely hast sat upon a thousand hallmotes during thy long lyf. But if you do not remember, I do. The wind was bitter that day, so we rustics stood inside the church. Cellarer, you were seated at the juror's table by the altar, stiff-back't and ready to begin. Lamentably, the same could not be said for Thomas the Bailiff, the last person to enter church.

Thomas had never attended a hallmote since his arrival in the village, so for many it was their first real sighting of the man. It was a sight fewe forgot. I be reminded of a verse about the Fell Wraith I heard sung by a Gatesheade Gleeman. His description of that heinous creature be goodly surrogate for any I might lend to the Bailiff—

> *Blaaaaa-ded bone,*
> *Priiiiiiiiick-ing flesh,*
> *Haaaaaaaaa-ggard pale,*
> *Raaaaaaaan-cid stench.*
> *The siiiiiiiiiick-ened wits,*

And eyes.
The eyes.
Drowwwwwwwn-ded in their,
Puuuuuuuuur-pled pits...

...From my
position at the back of church, I watch't Thomas stagger
towards the jurors' table. His hair lank o'er his visage. Pit upon
pit upon pit speckling the scarred latticeworks of his cheeks,
and the flesh of his temples were twin, churned horrors.
Taking his seat next to the Cellarer, he groaned as if his very
bones pained him. Cellarer—Hugh—you gave Thomas the hard
eye as the Clerk unwinded his roll in anticipation of business.

Of which, friends, there was much.

All that morn, the church rang not with the strange sounds
of Latin Mass, nor the hush't prayers and repeated names of
Segerston's dead languishing in Purgatory, but with corporeal
accusation and disagreement. Simon Nash had let his cows
trample Laurence Bigge's winter wheat. John Aycock accused
John Newcomb of malicious infringement upon two roods
of his land. Elyas Greene denounce't Maurice Spratling for
filching a bushel of barley from his outhouse, while Maurice
countered this was his right, as he had paid Elyas four groats
to repair his fences by the feast of Saint Matthias, which Elyas
had not done. Insensible with ale, Geoffrey Fitt had brok Peter
Jepson's sneck, for he believed Peter had defamed his wyf.
Beatrice Bone sold rotted cheese to Margaret Cullop. Matilda
Lodes slandered her sister-in-law Sabine, calling her a stronge
whore and fornicatrix in the presence of Stephen the Miller
and many others grinding their grains.

On and on it went, this spewing recrimination. Not so

long ago, these folk had been, if not mates, then of tolerable acquaintance. But friends, I ask you to resist judgment. These were no idle rustics taking advantage of a reclusive Bailiff to slacken in their affairs. Many of those entered into the court roll that day were goodly, hard-working souls...but the failed harvest weighed heavy. A second ruinous reap would destroy them. And so the social cloth of Segerston, caught upon the thorn of privation, began to unwind.

Though why ought that be thy concern, Cellarer? You could not trouble thyself with low intrigues 'twixt the Lord Sacrist's villeins. Thus, when one of the accused attempted to argue his case to thee, you did correct him.

I am not here today to arbitrate, you said, but to lend the authority of the Bishop of Durham. It is in his interest we all toil. Verdicts shall be decided by the jurors of this village, for they know its peoples and workings. The Bailiff will also provide rulings. Thomas, I trust you hast learn't much in thy tyme here?

Thomas' mumbled response caused thine lips, Cellarer, to press white. In dede, throughout that hallmote you did coax the Bailiff to bring his authority to bear upon the court, only for the man to defer to the jurors tyme and again as they meted out punishments. And, friends, how many punishments! Even as the church bell pealed Terce, we were far from done, and it was close to Evensong when, finally, my father was called.

Said the juror Denis Daunt, *Of what be this man Henry Payne accused?*

Ralf spoke. *Failing to harrow three furloughs of the Lord's demesne...*

But, Friends, my father was not at fault. His two oxen had been needed to plough elsewhere upon the demesne, and his only horse was engaged in harrowing his own holdings.

97

Crows were eating the seed he had sown there, and tarrying even another day in harrowing them o'er would have see them ruined. So Henry had woken in deepest night to work his own acres, for to be ready with his horse upon the Lord's lands by Prime. But that horse—never hath there lived such a stubborn and ill-starred beast. It refused to be driven at night, meaning Da was tardy for his demesne duties. All this Da tried explaining to the court, but he did stumble up...

...upon his

words...

...Excuse my emotion, friends. My father was a quiet man much given to inwardness. So, to stand there afore the village—afore thee, Cellarer—to defend his honest name, well, I ache to think on it.

As I ache to tell what happened next.

While the jurors discuss't his transgressions, my father could look nowhere but the stone floor of the church. When given the opportunity to say a final word in defence, it took all his strength to raise his head and speak.

I be pulled irrevocably in twain, said he. *I cannot farm my land and the Lord's land both. If I farm his demesne, I shall not have food enough for my family. Nor can I purchase what I do not grow, for its cost be high and the price of my grain kept low.*

His voice leak't away. Cellarer, you turned to Thomas.

Bailiff, what say you?

Thomas roused himself, though his mind was clearly upon some internal torture and not the case at hand.

Cellarer, said Thomas, *the Reeve is better positioned to pass comment upon this villein, for he hath known him many a year.*

Cellarer, thy sigh was audible to the back row.

So be it. Reeve?

Ralf cleared his throat. The usual coarseness of his voice was replace't by a servile tone none had heard afore. I believe even the man's hair was rake't.

Noble Cellarer, said the Reeve, *it be with great regret you waste thy tyme with low business such as this. Many villeins work all we can for the Lord Sacrist, but, alas, there be others who mock the pryde the rest of us take in our duty. Henry Payne be one such man. As Reeve, I cajole and entreat him to embrace his customary duties, but he refuses. I have failed him, and thee also. Forgive me, sir.*

Cellarer, you gave a slight nod. The jurors conferred, then Denis Daunt stood.

The hallmote fines Henry Payne two shillings, proclaimed he.

NAY! cried my father.

Beside me, Mam clung to Christopher. Both look't in disbelief at Da, this habitually meek man now raging afore none other than the Cellarer himself.

I cannot! yelled Henry. *I cannot be defamed and remain silent! I be no tare!*

Rustic, you said, Cellarer. *Counsel thyself.*

My father did not. *Cellarer, I say again—I be no tare! I work myself to BONE, only for mine toils to multiply. The Reeve—that man there, Ralf Deepslough—be fain corrupt. He shields his friends from demesne labours, to the disadvantage of his enemies, of which I be chief. And this jury be likewise rotten. They burden demesne obligations upon those with whom they quarrel.*

Defamer! bellowed Denis Daunt.

Base lies! cried Ralf.

Not lies! roared Henry, loudest of all. *That I be o'erburdened be no lie! Cellarer, Segerston hath too much land, and too fewe villeins.*

This be why villeins continue to flee. By the Rood, things be so bad that the notion sore tempts me also. And I be not the only bonded man who feels thus.

He turned to the gathered villeins, to a man he knew well— one William Turley.

Bill, said Da, *be that not true?*

I be content with my labour, replied William.

Father found Roger Applebottom, with whom he had once played amiable games of baggammon. Roger could not meet my father's eye.

I do not wish flee, said Roger. *God made us villein for this purpose.*

Henry, you fukkit rabble-rouser! screamed a voice in the crowd.

Howled another, *Unshriven Lollard!*

Aye, his wyf practices thumbnail sorcery upon her bairn, spoke a third, *for to discourse with Demons.*

And a poisoner, added a fourth.

Nay! cried someone in their defence. *The Paynes be decent folk. True!*

Fie! Then why hast YOU not help't them with their ploughshare?

The hallmote collapse't into tumult, and only brought to order by you, Cellarer, hammering the table for silence. When it came, you address't Thomas.

Bailiff, is what Henry Payne says true? How many villeins have fled the manor?

Thomas turned to Denis Daunt. *How—*

I address thee, Bailiff, said the Cellarer. *How many?*

Thomas grew paler still. He opened his gob, but no words issued.

Four, sir, said Ralf. *I believe four.*

Cellarer, you mastered thy rage at the Bailiff, for the village was discordant enough without public chastisement of its alleged leader. Instead, you made an example of my father.

Henry Payne, is it?

Yes, Cellarer.

You attempt to convince thine fellow villeins to reject their ancient demesne obligations to the Lord Sacrist? Putting false ideas on fleeing into their heads?

My father became white. *Nay, sir. I...I only—*

You only incite rebellion. If you revere Wat Tyler so, I can arrange for thy head to follow his likewise upon a spyke. Is that thy wish?

Fear robbed Da of words.

As I thought, you said, Cellarer. *Jurors—uphold this man's two shillings, and double it for his sedition...*

42

...Cellarer, four shillings was nigh a quarter of my father's annual earnings. But Segerston was a wilde horse refusing the bridle, so you crack't whip. Henry Payne's punishment was the wound you hadst no choice but to deliver, though, Hugh, mayhap, you truly *did* think Da to be another dangerous Wat Tyler? And believed likewise the insults spat at him that day? *Rabble-rouser! Unshriven Lollard!* Only you can say, Cellarer. Yet, speaking of Lollardy provokes a memory ye may all find gratifying...

...This was some years gone now, mayhap around the recommencement of war with the French, following those decades of truce. Pearl Eye and myself had arrived in Pontefreyt, at the southern-most swoop of our annual gyre. Pontefreyt be a gay enough town, and usually paid a decent purse, but the people gathered to market that day were not disposed to our strumming. A tall stage had been erected in the square, upon which stood six wooden frames, each the height of a man and more.

All present knew what they were for.

The only questions were *who*.

And *why*.

Anon, both mysteries were answered when a bell rang out. The crowd split apart so the Sheriff and his men could lead out six manacled Lollards in their infamous russet robes an—

...Aye, Mercers, jeer away! And believe me, there came many more from the crowd that day! Though I do own, some quarters did remain silent—in sympathy or dread I know not—as the heretical Priests were hauled onto the stage and tied to the frames. The Sheriff's Clerk read out their Lollard crime—translation of the book of Psalms into the English tongue. This was grievous sin, for God hath decreed the Bible remain in Latin, to be read aloud in church only by trained Priests capable of its explanation. Why, if *any* lettered wight could read the Word of God at his own leisure—in his own *hame*—how could it not reduce God's majesty by association? And worse, what if such commoners misunderstood God's Word? Got harmful ideas about himself and his station—that he be other to what God made him—then began thinking thoughts a Priest would hath protected him from ever entertaining? What if he then pass't these bent learnings onto even lower men?

To *rustics?*

I shudder to think!

Addressing the crowd, the Sheriff said the six Lollards

would receive one hundred and one-half lashes—a blow for each Psalm they wish't desecrate. Having torn off their robes, the Sheriff's men lash't away at the Lollards' naked backs with long scourges. Some Lollards howled in anguish and others stayed silent. Gore flew for all. On and on it went, until even those in attendance who despised Lollardy began moaning. Eventually, the Sheriff's men lowered their dripping whips... though only for as long as it took to turn the flayed Lollards o'er upon the frames so that their fronts could be lain siege to. Beside me, a woman swooned as one Lollard's nypple was torn away. Ribs began shewing white 'neath brutalised meat, the stage flooding with viscera. A wayward stryke rip't open a Lollard cheek from lip to ear. In truth, I felt we were in Hell, where tyme hath ended and torment endures eternal—but it was Pontefreyt still, and when the Sheriff's men reach't one hundred-and-one-half lashes, they step't back in silence.

The Sheriff was silent.

The crowd silent.

The six Lollard men silent too, though in truth they no longer resembled men. In their places—six raw heaps of hack't meat like the carcasses of apprentice Butchers. And like carcasses, they were cut down and dragged away.

When they were gone, animation returned to the crowd. I turned to where I thought Pearl Eye had been standing, but he was gone. It was many hours later that I found him again, supping in some dim tavern.

Pearl, you left? Did you see what happened to those Lollards?
Pearl finish't his cup, reach't for another.
They were torn to shreds, said I. *And you saunter off to sup?*
Down his gullet went the ale.
Why do you ignore me?

103

The ale be goode, said Pearl. *Sit down if it pleases. Or not. I do not give a pea.*

Miserable auld bugger. Why—

A lightning fork struck mine wits, and I understood his enmity. See, I had seen Pearl undress't many tymes, and knew the deep scars across his back and buttocks. Pearl had telt me the culprit was his father, Gervase, the high-rank't Gleeman whose ruination had, for his son, manifested in nightly beatings and the loss of an eye. In dede, Gervase's violence only stop't when Pearl awoke one morn to find his father dead on his pallet, choke't upon his own spew. Pearl then took Gervase's psaltery and left their hovel, walking for days 'til he came to some small hamlet. A fayre was in progress, so he stood upon a tree stump, shouldered his instrument and played. Quickly did a crowd congregate around the skinny one-eyed lad who sang with a force to quail all other Gleeman thereabout. Who bent songs to *his* will. By the tyme he had finish't, his voice was blown and his cheeks wet with tears he remembered shedding not. The crowd cheered and threw coins at his stump while two jilted Gleemen look't on envious. Said the one to his mate, *Who be this pearl-eyed churl?* Thus, in the next town, my friend stood afore a new crowd and said, *How fare ye? I be the Gleeman Pearl Eye!* And from that day on, that was his only name. Pearl once telt me it was the only name that fit. One that pierce't a hole through to the core of him, so whatever roiled inside could spill free...

43

...But enough of Pearl and Lollards and

tales within tales! Let us attend to lashes of a different sort—
the spoken kind. Specifically, dear Cellarer, those you subjected
the Bailiff to immediately after hallmote that day.

Greatly anguish't by my father's punishment, I had slip't
away from church and into the trees of the heugh. Behind the
rotted trunk of some long-fallen oak, I wept. But by degrees,
mine mewlings ended, and I was brushing the leaf fall from my
tunic when voices reach't my ear. They spoke urgently from the
top of the heugh, in the direction of the manor house. Creeping
nearer, I espied thee, Cellarer, unleashing upon Thomas a
verbal lashing to rival the physikal beating the Sheriff's men
delivered unto those Pontefreyt Lollards. Evensong was past,
the sky near wrung of light, so I crept behind the croft wall and
opened mine ears.

Fie! you cried, Cellarer. *What a fukkit farce that was!*

Thomas the Bailiff made no answer.

You dare not look upon me? How you heap insult upon ignominy!

Though I could not see, Thomas must hath raised his bleary
eyes to thee.

Cellarer, said Thomas, *earlier hallmotes proceeded with order.
This was an exception.*

The only exception was thy presence at it.

The previous Bailiff's death left much in disarray, replied
Thomas. *Though I wish chair every hallmote, oftentymes my work
busies me elsewhere.*

*Oh, you hast been busy! I smell the claret on thee from here!
The Refectorian at the cathedral, he tells me six wine kegs hast thee
taken delivery of since thy arrival here. Six!*

I entertain, Thomas said.

*Folly and idleness, that is what you entertain. They are
thine year-around guests. In dede, is that not why you are here?*

Languishing amid these reeking rustics, and not a Monk or Man of Law like thine brothers? I confess, Thomas, when the Sacrist told me of his plan to install thee as Bailiff, I told him I did not think thee capable. But the Sacrist is a wise man. In thy defence, he quoth the Parable of the Unforgiving Servant. I trust thee recalls the lesson?

Cellarer, shall we step inside to discuss such things?

Ignoring this, Cellarer, you telt the Bailiff how Peter the Apostle had believed his own generosity in forgiving up to seven tymes those who sinned against him, 'til Christ said Nay, Peter, not seven, but *seventy tymes seven.* Cellarer, you then said the Sacrist had wish't for him—for Thomas—to be granted the same number of chances at redemption.

I understand, said Thomas.

Today's hallmote persuades me otherwise. If those rustics forget their place, all is lost. One failed harvest, and these wights threaten to become ungovernable. Two in succession shall be the deathblow, and when they have naught left to lose...

Cellar, I tell thee I understand.

Then why do I see so many wasted acres?

I lack men. I wage what cottars I can, but they now demand such high wages.

High wages? you said, Cellarer. *For what? Pulling weeds and carting shite? Increase their coin and cottars from other manors will demand the same from their own Lords. You unleash forces that can never be tamed. Pay a ditch-digger the same purse as a guild man, and soon the guild man covets MY purse. Mark me, Thomas—it is a dangerous world where a rustic and an intelligent man earn equal wage. Where shall it lead? Do I sit down to supper with my hound? Celebrate Whitsuntide with my best pig?*

The truth remains, said Thomas, *that we require more hands.*

Not cottar hands. Cottars are feckless and unreliable—that is why God made them cottars. Bonded men, Thomas. You need bonded men.

Villeins are also lacking.

I dare say that hath something to do with the number you allow to abscond. Four since I was last here! Where are they now?

Mayhap Thomas shook his head. All I know be that thee, Cellarer, spoke next.

Every tyme one of those churls flees and is not brough to heel, it emboldens the others likewise. Each one lost shrinks the Sacrist's purse, which shrinks the church's pur—

Enough! cried Thomas. *I beseech thee, shame me no further!*

Crouch'd as I was behind the wall, the nithering wind brought me the sound of the Bailiff's snotty blubbering and vomitous retches. Cellarer, you waited in silence 'til Thomas ended his display.

I wish encourage thee, you said, *not shame thee. The Sacrist awaits my report upon Segerston's progress. It is in thy power to decide what I tell him...and what he then says to Duncan.*

You need not invoke my father's name, said Thomas.

Silence, then, from both men.

When you were dying of pox, you said, eventually, *God spared thy lyf so you could do goode with it. Thus, if you do not do goode, you reject thy lyf, and reject God. And that, Thomas, that is the only unpardonable sin. Matthew twelve-thirty two, "And whosoever speaketh a word against the Son of Man, it shall be forgiven him, but whosoever speaketh against the Holy Ghost, it shall not be forgiven him, neither in this world, neither in the world to come."*

I do not speak against God, sir.

"Neither in the world to come." Thomas, you risk eternal damnation. You risk Hell.

Cellarer—Hugh—the harvest shall not fail. Now, excuse me, I must attend my work.

The manor door creak't open. Cellarer, you called out to the Bailiff afore it shut.

Seventy-tymes seven, you said.

Cellarer?

Seventy-tymes seven. Can you tell me the resultant figure?

Forgive me, said Thomas. *It hath been a long day and I cannot bring it to mind.*

Cellarer, you sighed. *It behoves a Bailiff to remember his arithmetic, but no matter. The number is four hundred and ninety. And having learned of thine exploits—thine disputes, debts, and disorder—I believe thine total transgressions fast approach this number. What lies in store beyond it? I know not, save God shall close his ears to thee.*

Thomas did not speak.

But do not close thine ears to this, Thomas—not one more villein leaves this land...

44

...Cellarer, after you left to fulfil obligations upon the Sacrist's six other manors, I saw the sobering effect thine words had on Thomas Harpour. He took up a manner more befitting a Bailiff, and was seen upon his horse in the fields, o'erseeing the ploughing and sowing, harrowing and folding. Long-delayed repairs to cottages and outbuildings were undertaken. The Bailiff was also witness't to the south of Segerston, amid the wasted lands. What this meant, nobody quite knew, but the villagers had other worries to occupy them.

Despite the additional work, there had been no increase in men to do it. Everyone able to be in the field was thus so. For villeins, this meant Ralf Deepslough could less easily take the obligations from his allies and put them onto his enemies, but the Reeve still contrived to give Henry Payne the most arduous tasks. This he did again during May's unseasonable coldness, when Thomas commanded Ralf cut more fyrewood for the manor, and the Reeve had only one man in mind for that labour...

45

...Sacrist, I was with Da in thine woods that day, standing back as he buried his axe into the trees there. He had been working in the fields since afore Lauds, without rest and only meagre pottage for sustenance, and his weariness was plain. This fatigue, in league with the cold benumbing his fingers, caused the axe shaft to slip from his frozen hands, the iron head striking the trunk and doubling back, the whetted blade sinking deep into his foot...

...Queer, but neither of us moved. We both stared down at the axe jutting out of his flesh. A wildness in Da's face as he look't to me. Eyes huge, lips peeled.

Son, said he. *Be I Elm or Poplar?*

I laugh't, though not from mirth. With a sharp cry, Da pulled the blade free and bound the steaming gush with strips torn from his tunic.

Back hame, we inspected the damage. The axe had cleaved

crossways across his foot, severing two toes clean and leaving a third dangling by strings. Mam cleaned the wound and applied a poultice, but inflammation set in anon, then the stench of decay. Yet even as he sickened, my father took himself into the fields—hobbling upon a crutch. What choice had he? Declaring himself too poorly to perform his demesne duties would raise questions if he was then seen working his own holdings, and he could not let what crops he had fall to waste. For you were correct, Cellarer, when you said a second failed harvest would ruin Segerston. The deathblow, I believe you said.

As that axe did bring death to Da, for he was gone within the week.

While he lay dying, Mam sent me to fetch Father Bell. I was afeared he would not come after what happened during Holy Week, but come he did, with his Chaplin, pyx, candles, and the painted statue of the Madonna. Aglitter with sweat, Da drifted like ashes 'twixt waking and slumber. I fretted he would die afore Father Bell could provide for him shrift and housel, and so save him from eternal damnation.

But God was with us. At the sight of Father Bell lighting candles about his pallet, father groaned to shew his mind still clung on for what had next to be done...

46

...Friends, the final moments afore death be the most fraught a man lives. Listen to this succinct couplet—

Live well, die never.

...For in those dwindling breaths where lyf teeters upon the rim of two worlds, grave danger abounds. Demons perch beyond the candle glow, waiting for some fatal error by either Priest or parishioner in enactment of final rites, so that they may drag the dying person's unshriven, unhoused soul to Hell. Mam oftentymes said it was her greatest comfort that mine middle siblings had both died well. It was why she said her daily Paternosters and Aves, so when the tyme came we would all pass from this lyf to meet again in Purgatory, afore one day journeying onwards to Heaven's endless bliss.

So, ye can imagine her relief when, as her hysband neared death, all started well. Father Bell shrived Da and listened to his whispered confession—the particulars of which remain 'twixt those two men—and unburdened his soul of sin. Thus shriven, Father Bell annealed Da's head and feet with oil in preparation of housel. From his pyx, he took the sacred body of Christ and tried to place it upon Da's tongue, but Da was fading. Mam clutch't her breast.

Father, she said. *Father, he cannot swallow.*

The Priest brok Christ's body into a cup of wine, but did not pour it into Da's mouth. Instead, he shook Da by the shoulder.

Henry, said Father Bell. *Does my voice reach thee?*

Da groaned in the affirmative.

Henry, the lead in the south window of the church needs replacement. Two shillings ought suffice.

Da opened his fearful eyes. Father Bell took his hand.

For thy benefit, said the Priest. *To weight the scale of judgment further in thy favour. Squeeze my hand, Henry, if I have permission to take that price from thine chattels.*

Struggling for breath, Da lock't eyes upon the chalice in Father Bell's hand, the cup of wine in which floated his Host and salvation. The Priest look't about himself.

Hellspawn crowds near! said he. *Two shillings, afore the fiends o'errun us!*

My father squeezed his hand, and with that, Father Bell engaged upon Da's final piece of worldly business—Ralf Deepslough.

You quarrelled with him, said Father Bell. *But holding onto such things shall condemn thee. Forgive his injuries against thee, Henry.*

A tear fell upon Da's cheek.

Weep not, man! Do you not hear that wet gobbling? Those are Demons wanting to pluck thy soul away! And they shall, Henry, if you do not forgive Ralf Deepslough.

Do as he says, cried Alice. *Henry, I beg thee.*

In agony, Da look't from his wyf back to Father Bell.

Henry, do you forgive Ralf Deepslough all he hath done to thee?

My father squeezed Father Bell's hand, and the Priest was able to pour the Host into Da's mouth. He spluttered upon Christ's body, but did swallow him down as Father Bell murmured *commendatio animae,* granting my father leave to die a goode death. Which he did immediately...

...

...I shall

never forget what Father Bell did...

...Aye, Sacrist, no *truer*
representative of thy institution could thee hope to find...

47

...They buried Da two days later. Fewe people came. Then
two days after *that*, a hallmote was called. Christopher was
of age, so our father's holdings and obligations pass't to him.
My brother paid entrance fee to the land, and a heriot of one
of our oxen due to thee, Sacrist. Christopher argued forcibly
to commute to ten shillings the heriot of his second-best ox—
which was to be given to Father Bell—for it would leave him
with no oxen at all. This request was granted, so Christopher knelt afore the Bailiff to grasp the white end of the rod,
swearing fealty that he would not allow the Lord Sacrist's land
to turn to waste, nor his buildings fall to decay.

Thus done, Christopher become head of our family.

And I his apprentice. As Da had taught him, he thus taught
me to guide our single ox. My brother's lessons were terse, and
though I tried speaking to him of other things, he did not wish
converse. For some tyme, he had been courting a villein lass in
the village. They loved each other strongly, and it was expected
they would be wed. But since evil rumours of the Paynes had
been noised about, she had cooled on him. After Da's death,
Christopher had gone to call and this lass informed him she
no longer accepted his love. Whether this was the will of her
father, who had sickened from Alice's ale, or the lass herself
swayed fickle by village chatter, my brother knew not. His only
certainty was that his future—dreams of his own hame, his

own bairns—were burn't away. Christopher fell to brooding, and while we toiled upon the Sacrist's demesne, he push't himself beyond endurance, mayhap in futile bid to outpace his anguish. His rage...

...He took sick with fever, hectic and burning. Mam could do naught to cool him, for as soon as she place't the cold rag upon his brow did it fain catch like kindling. Decades later, with the help of Lancaster Lambert's medical texts, I did form my brother's diagnosis—I read how anger heats the vital spirit residing in the chambers of the heart, spreading fatal fyres through the veins. To the same effect, great sorrow curdles to rage within the soul. In Christopher's case, did sorrow begat anger, or anger sorrow? All I know be that once more Mam bid me fetch Father Bell, who, after securing another shilling for the south window of the parish church, provided my brother with a goode death.

And we buried him in the same grave as Da...

48

...I was not of age to inherit, so the hallmote bade Mam take guardianship of our smallholdings and demesne obligations until that tyme came. She grasp't the same white rod as her eldest boy, now dead, had done scant weeks afore—as her dead hysband had done—and swore fealty. She paid entrance to the land and her second ox was taken as heriot, leaving her with none. From the bottom of sorrow's deep pit, she found voice to protest this, only for Thomas to inform her she may purchase the beast back at her leisure.

Leisure, Bailiff? I have none.

Well, that shall hasten thy purchase, said Thomas.

In the corner of my eye, Ralf grinned gleeful. But his spite melted like tallow as Thomas spoke to the gathered village.

As I now require haste from each villein here, because from today ye all receive additional demesne. The lands to the south, which fell to waste during the Pestilence, total two hundred acres. Too long have they been abandoned to lossmaking. So today, I allocate to each bonded family their portion, to be work't to profit alongside thine current duties to the Sacrist.

Discontent, thick and lusty, noised about as Thomas address't the jury.

I leave it to you to divvy things justly. Clerk, record all in the manor roll.

As the Bailiff pass't me, our eyes met. It was I who turned away. When he was gone, the village burst into bitter accusation. I stayed close to Mam as she led us through the thresh. I look't back only once, wish't I had not. For it was Ralf Deepslough's gaze I met, and his smile had returned...

49

...May wore on—a month where squall follows sunbeam within the span of a single morn. The turbulent climate fit the mood of the villagers all out in the fields. Where once the free and unfree, the landed and landless, the rich and impover-ish't, had work't side by side in tolerable accord, now mounting privation levered up into clear view the disparity that had always been there.

For to work those additional acres of wasted demesne, the Bailiff waged all of Segerston's cottars and freemen, putting them to work alongside his villeins. But the freemen had increase't their rents in competition of Duncan Harpour's Mercer apprenticeship, so their cottar-tenants work't harder for less reward. Many of them left the village—free cottars having that right—in search of cheaper dwellings. This exodus set into motion a chain of recrimination...

...For the shortage of cottars caused those who remained to agitate for higher wages if they were to continue working for the Lord Sacrist...

...Which angered the villeins, for why should those greedy, grasping cottars demand more coin for the same work *they* must do gratis...?

...That freeman landlords might avoid entirely by simply increasing his rents...?

...*Fie!* grutch't the villeins. These churls—freeman and cottar alike—how did they have the *culls* to bemoan their lots? In dede, every additional moment a villein was made to spend upon the Lord's demesne because some idle cottar or landed freemen chose not to, that was an additional moment the villein was kept from his own holdings...

...Thus, friends, much as the court of then-King

116

Richard was at that tyme tearing itself apart, so Segerston in June 1397 was split into bitter factions. Not even Ralf could ignore the added burdens upon himself, thus he was doubly strict with Mam and me. He walk't our portions of wasted demesne to ensure we turned the agreed-upon length, not a pace less. This we did. Though without oxen, Mam was force't to rely upon our remaining beast to plough and harrow.

The dray horse.

I spoke of this foul thing earlier, but only briefly for the belligerency of that hoof't bastard stokes my blood even now. It nickered and stamp't at the mere sight of the plough, and much tyme each day was squandered in harnessing. Out upon the land, its progress was not steady as an ox, but fitful and wayward. Mam and I wrestled endlessly with the beast to keep it from thundering off to the horizon like the Black Prince's warhorse at Crécy. Aye, that fukkit animal wrung us dry— two souls already fain wearied afore we rose from our pallet each morn. But, still, I was grateful for the work. Labour cares naught of grief, and I wish't it render me too spent to feel the enormity of what I had lost.

But alas, friends, our exertions were not confined to the physikal realm. Nay, Mam and I did also toil upon an altogether more Divine plane. Kneeling beside her in church, long after Evensong each night, the two of us weary and filthy from our field labours, feverishly did we pray. We prayed not only for the departed souls of Da and Chirstopher to pass speedily through the torments of Purgatory, but for the souls of mine other dead siblings likewise. Sibyl and Robert were their names. Ma telt me stories—as Da and Christopher had when they still lived— such wonderful stories. Like how Robert had nurse't a crow with an ill wing 'til it gained the sky once more. And Sibyl,

117

how she had capered upon her hands to rival any Saltatrix. These tales delighted but also saddened me, for in truth, I did not remember my brother and sister, so they...

 ...they did
not...

 ...they never felt *real*...

 ...Thus, when I went to church to pray for their souls—when I repeated their names as Father Bell read them from the parish Bede-Roll—I did not *see* them in my mind, and so failed them in my heart. Amid my grief, guilt did grow. And I wish't then, as I wish now, to possess proper means to commemorate them. To atone for my forgetting by keeping their names upon the lips of hundreds— nay, thousands—and so hasten their souls towards their final rests.

But I was a poor childe, friends, and could not.

As I be a poor Gleeman now...

50

 ...Which puts me in mind of an event that occurred mayhap fifteen years ago, when neither Pearl nor I were young men any longer. We had arrived in the city of Hull for the feast of Corpus Christi, where the Silversmith guild there intended to perform the Last Judgment in the square by the Church of the Holy Trinity. The guild needed music, so waged us to add our strumming to their words and deeds. As I recall, our fortunes had been brought lower than usual, granting us little choice.

Of all religious plays that guilds about the land put on annually for the benefit and instruction of the lower orders, Christ's return be most often performed. The Silversmiths had spared no expense in their preparations. Mounted upon a horse-pulled wagon was the canniest stage I have ever seen—aye, Mercers, even cannier than your own—for it did possess a functioning Hellmouth, the yawning jaws of which moved by dint of some ingenious mechanism. Costumed Devils, Demons, and Wraiths would spew from this orifice and swarm the unshriven sinners left behind after Judgment Day. Aye, a terrifying thing, friends, as was the music Pearl and I composed to herald the arrival of those Fiends.

For days we engaged in the perfection of this play, and were thus privy to its many practice repetitions. Some Hull Silversmiths took roles as Goode Souls and Bad, each stating their case to Lord Jesus upon the world's final day and, well, friends, I believe you Mercers did put on this same play in Durham some years gone, so I shall not tarry in explanation of its content. Suffice to say, during their practicing, the Silversmiths would often leave off their lines to jape and jangle, with one merry source of debate being this—on the day the world really *did* end, who among their patrons might be Heaven-bound, and who gulp't to Hell? Much horseplay then followed o'er such-and-such a customer, the notorious welsher of debts; some Lord who, in exchange for six engraved candlesticks, had promise't payment of a bevy of juicy pheasants from his woods, only for the delivered birds to be fain mealy.

I paid scant attention to such blether until the Smiths' talk turned to their own deaths and preparations for Purgatory.

For just as the parish Bede-Roll read out each Sunday allows the living to repeat the names of the dead and so lessen their Purgatorial sentence, so rich men arrange additional ways to ensure swiftest passage into Heaven eternal.

The Master Silversmith playing Jesus, he telt his guildmates of the will he had just ink't for to leave seven hundred-and-one-half-pounds of wax to the Holy Trinity church, to be lit upon the Paschal Sepulchre each Eastertide and upon his tomb during feasts. Another Smith, dress't as a Goblin, had set aside one-hundred-and-one-half gold nobles for ten Priests to sing Mass in his name for the next fifty years. Jesus and the Goblin compared arithmetic to see which method resulted in the most reduce't stay in Purgatory, with the Goblin emerging victorious for nigh on three thousand fewer years would his soul languish in agony there. This figure, however, was bested by a third Smith—Angel wings lash't to his spine—who spoke of the rustic he had waged to make foreign pilgrimage in his stead, to the Santiago de Compostela in Galicia, to pay homage to the Holy Prepuce of Christ. Said the Angel, to be safe, he had instructed this rustic to travel thence to Holland and Saxony and the other Shrines about the world where that Sainted foreskin was said also to reside. By his calculation, the Shrine badges his rustic wayfarer would return to him from those places would stryke close to seven thousand years from his brutal suffering. Together, the Silversmiths then mock't this waged-pilgrim for his poverty and ugliness, afore turning to rumours the Pope was soon to offer indulgences worth *fourteen thousand years* to those visiting the Basilica of Saint Peter. And they were just agreeing to send men to Rome on their behalf to collect it for them, when a clanging chord rang out. All turned as one body in the direction of its source—Pearl Eye.

Gleeman! bellowed Goblin Silversmith. *What are you about? About?* said Pearl.

If that is the quality of thy playing, said Angel, *we have waged the wrong man.*

Pearl flash't teeth most horribly. *Waging men—that does seem thy speciality.*

Explain thyself, Gleeman, said Jesus.

My Heavenly Lord, replied Pearl, *you would not enjoy that.*

I knew well my friend's caustic tone. Things would end badly if I did not get him away anon. This I did with much apology and pledge that, come performance day, Pearl and I would fulfil our musical obligations to perfection.

For thy friend's sake, spoke Jesus, *pray it is true...*

51

...Well, friends, that day arrived and Pearl did not. Tyme slipping away, I search't Hull top to bottom, finding him fain cockeyed in some louse-ridden tavern. I let fly at him.

Why torture me so, Pearl? Look at mine hairs—I be gone grey with thee!

You be grey, Mother, because you be auld. And I aulder.

Come away now, and we can still get to the performance.

Pearl poured the dregs of several ale cups into one, and drank.

One hundred and one half gold nobles, said he.

What?

Fukkit nobles that dog-frigging Goblin gave some singing Priests. More coin than a villein makes in thirty lyftymes. And his mate—him what thinks he got seven thousand years scored off Purgatory by waging some wight to make pilgrimage in his stead...

Shall you do this in every town?

Do what, Mother?

Aggrieve thyself at our employers for their wealth.

Fine, Mother. I also begrudge those Smiths for they smelt like thine fukkit feet.

Pearl, this be no tyme for japes.

Japes? How about this for a jape—I once knew a lad who got waged to walk another's pilgrimage to Rome. Some chinless wyf of a merchant who long ago had bent her penny to Saint Lawrence, to visit his bones there. But did she cross the seas? Like shite. She dithered twenty more years 'til she wobbled worse than a milk pudding. So they paid this rustic lad six months' wage to go in her stead. He needed the purse, the lad, for he had three bairns to feed, a fourth on the way. So off he went...

And?

And bandits slit his throat in the Alps.

God's bones, man, what be thy poynte?

That the Final Judgment be a rotten play in Silversmith hands. That their fancy wagon and costumes be no work of charity, for rich men open their purse only if they think it speeds them through Purgatory. And how many others who cannot afford it be then inspired to imitation? How many starving wights take bread from the gobs of their living bairns because they be telt it better feeds their dead?

Pearl, you speak as if this be some new revelation.

Purgatory? Mayhap it be so. For some say there be no mention of it in the Bible. I would not know, as I do not speak Latin and so must trust some fukkit Priests who says elsewise.

Pearl...you deny the existence of Purgatory?

I only say such a place makes a rich man arrogant, and a poor man poorer.

We be poor, Pearl. The Silversmith wage shall redress that, but only if you come now.

And what then?

And what then, what?

Mother, does it not tire thee?

What, Pearl?

This. The endless walking from place to place. The barns we sleep in. The empty purses. This "freedom" you and I possess—free to starve, free to freeze.

But free to choose where we do either, said I, but with trepidation. For some tyme, I had notice't melancholy in my friend, but never had he spoken so bleakly. And my distress grew when Pearl lowered his head into an ale puddle on the table and began to sing—

> *Mother, what have I made of myself?*
> *Mother, I beg thee—what be my use?*
> > *How did I ever*
> > *Fashion my passion*
> > *When did I twist it,*
> > *Into a noose...?*

...When he finish't, some drynkers raised mocking cheer. Ignoring them, I touch't my auld friend's shoulder.

Pearl?

He sat up, ale dripping from his sneck.

Pay me no mind, said he. *I be right.*

Pearl, you can speak thy mind to me.
Naught to speak, Mother. Let us go and play for the Silversmiths.
Truly?
Aye, he replied. *For we be Gleeman and that be our purpose.*
Always playing...

...We arrived to the square outside the
church just as the Silversmith wagon drew up. A large crowd
had gathered in anticipation of the end of the world. As Jesus,
Master Silversmith sat upon his white throne to judge the
dead by their living works. In this, I was reminded of the Day
of Doom painted upon the chancel arch in Segerston church,
of Father Bell's warnings that endless agony awaited those
who defied God's order. As I strummed, my mind went to my
mother. She had died a bad death without shrift and housel,
and was thus unable to enter into Purgatory. The thought of her
soul lost for all eternity, it hath never cease't paining me, and
though I sometymes managed to bury that truth in some deep,
unthinking part of myself, it be always there.

Always there.

Upon his Throne of Judgment, Silversmith Jesus praised the
souls he would save. For when he had first walk't the Earth,
the Goode Souls had clothed him when he was naked, fed him
when he starved. A grand speech it was, but as Christ spoke,
there came from Pearl's psaltery a high and whining note
which caused the Son of God to stumble o'er his words. Master
Silversmith look't evilly upon Pearl as—his goode eye pink
with ale—he unleash't another needling sequence. This Pearl
kept up throughout the play, troubling each Silversmith as they
performed, until all did seeth at him...

...Ah, friends! See this tear wet my white-whiskered cheek as I marvel anew at my auld friend! For how many of us born be able to do likewise? To unite Apostle and Demon, the Saved and the Damned thus...?

...Alas, Master Silversmith Jesus shared not my wonder. After the performance, we found him at his guildhall to request our wage and he threatened us with the Sheriff. I tried to negotiate a reduce't rate—enough to see us to the next town—but still drunk, Pearl cared naught for mediation.

Concession be futile, Mother, snarled he. *One who cheats himself into Heaven shall not think twice to cheat the likes of us.*

The Silversmith pulled off his false Jesus-whiskers with such fury that hairs clung higgle and piggle about his chops.

You call me a cheat, Gleeman, when YOU demand coin for duty unfulfilled?

Duty unfulfilled? Pearl laugh't. *Be it any different than waging some wight to traipse to Galicia for thee, to pay respect to a mouldy foreskin? Or slinging a near-ton of candle at the Bishop? Tell me, Smith, what be a soul's weight in wax?*

More than you can afford, said he. *For you, Gleeman, you create naught of perpetuity. Thy lyf, like thy art, be but a flatulence. A momentary stink upon the air! A feeble noi—*

Pearl drove his fist into Jesus' face, sending him sprawling, sneck spurting blood...

52

...Friends, what a caper we had
then! With Silversmith blows raining down upon us, we flew
from the guildhall into the dark streets and towards the trees
beyond Hull's city walls. In a moonlighted clearing, I spat
a bloody tooth into my palm. It was not the first I had lost
on Pearl's account, yet when I turned to him so that I might
impart that truth, I was *astonish't* to see him on his knees, face
sloughing in defeat as he muttered the Silversmith's final dart.

A momentary stink upon the air...

What? ask't I.

That's what he said of what I do...of who I be. Forgotten. Worthless.

Since when do you care what the likes of him thinks of thee?

Pearl hung his head.

Since for some years now, I have myself feared it to be true...

53

...And that, friends, was how we were banish't from Hull. I
repeat it to shew that not even Pearl was free of the fear of
being forgotten, for a forgotten soul be truly lost. Wealth saves
a rich man's soul from such a fate, while a poor man's community remembers him after he dies. Thus may ye think the whole
scheme perfect, but there be a terrible flaw...

...For what if
thy community decides to hurl thy soul into oblivion...?

...This very thing happened to Mam and I, when Segerston devised for us the most grievous punishment. Each Sunday, when Father Bell stood afore the altar to read the parish Bede-Roll of the dead, now all there gathered—each rustic man, woman, childe—refused to recite the name of any Payne. Not Da, Christopher, Robert, Sybil, nor any other of our blood, thus extending their Purgatorial torment with each snub. And it was *this* blow—not the endless toil, the heaping debts and blackest future—that did break Mam. Oftentymes, in the field or upon our pallet each night, she wept. I tried lifting her spirits by singing brightly, as I had done in the past, but she was too disconsolate to dance. To even smile. And could she be blamed? All us Paynes would scream the longest possible span in Purgatory, for when the last of us died, nobody living would be willing to remember our names in prayer. Nobody to light us even the shortest wick, for wax be that other crucial pillar of intervention on behalf of one's soul.

Aye, wax and tongues, friends. Wax and tongues...

...You, Mercer, sir. You there now supping thy wine—and I implore ye all to drynke up!—sir, I assume you hast ink't a will...

...Aye, very wise, sir. And in that will, hast you bequeathed a dedication of wax to thy guild's church of Saint Nicholas...

...Six hundred pounds, sir! How grand! Now, another man. You o'er there! The Mercer with the drooping whiskers. Aye, sir, you. When the tyme comes, how many Priest hast you waged to sing Mass in thy name...?

...A dozen Priests? That be even more than the Silversm—

...Now I hear grutchings among you. Friends, I mean no insolence! These benefits be not why ye joined the guild of Mercers. Of *course* not. Nay, ye did so for it was God's wish you spread the joy of finery to Durham's citizens. In dede, this be why the Mercers of Durham be the greatest guild in the city.

And why you, Walter, hadst once been so distraught to think you would never become part of it...

54

...Do you remember that day, Walter? I had gone to fetch water when those Deepslough brothers once more caught and beat me, smiting my water pail to gobbets. Miserable, I snivelled off to my usual spotte by the wall of the Bishop's deer park to weep mine eyes dry, which was when you appeared, Walter, as if you hadst been waiting for me. I had not know you were back from the grammar school. Nor why you also hadst tearful cheeks.

My da, you said, *he says the Mercer apprenticeship likely shall go to some other lad.*

Walter, I confess I wondered why this truth surprised thee. Thy father was but a minor freeman. Surely it was clear one better endowed would fill Thomas the Bailiff's purse and send their lad to Duncan Harpour? But hope be like ale, and bolsters wits if imbibed by the gallon. Sober realisation comes later, and with much paining.

By the wall that day, Walter, you spoke as you gazed morosely out upon the endless fells.

Never did you leap this wall into the Bishop's wildes.

Nor did you, replied I.

It was a game long-establish't 'twixt us, remember? The long hours we spent planning clandestine raids into the Bishop's lands, and not one second spent in their enactment.

Not then, anywise.

Such childish things no longer interest me, you said. *Mine imaginings transport me far beyond a mere deer park. I wish be a Mercer making journeys to London, Flanders, Venice. It was my heart's desire to see those places.*

Mayhap you still can. After all, you be a freeman.

Walter, I saw you did not believe me, for a poor freeman be worse off than a rich villein. You ask't me a question.

If you could travel to any place, where would it be?

I gave this some thought.

Herthepoll, said I.

Herthepoll? That be twenty miles from here?

My answer befuddled thee 'til I spoke of Mam's Granda, a man born in Herthepoll that she had loved greatly. It had always been her wish to visit his place of birth, and learn if anyone there still spoke of him.

Thus, said I, *Mam's wish be my own.*

Walter, you put thy arm about me.

God willing, he grants both our wishes.

Aye, Walter. God willing...

...Walter, those were the last words to pass 'twixt us until now. For not many days later,

Mam awoke me in the teeth of the night, and we fled Segerston with naught but a fardel upon our backs...

55

...So afeard was I that first night upon the roads, that not until pale dawn was unwinding low across the land did I dare ask our destination.

The sea, said Mam

We kept to the woods, travelling only at night and sleeping down the day. We nibbled stale maslin bread and whatever fungus grew in shaded hollows. When we saw bodies in transit, we cringed into brambles, lest they be Agents sent by Thomas to hunt us. Four or five days pass't likewise, and still no sea did we spy. We were lost, for Mam had never been much beyond Segerston's borders her entire lyf, and each step away from the place compounded her doubt and dread.

One twilight as we prepared to move, Mam put my thumb into her mouth and suck't it clean. Blowing upon it, she whispered queer words not even I, who spoke tolerable Latin, could comprehend.

Mam, what—

She squeezed my hand to silence me, reciting her spell once more. Then she held my thumb up to the dying day, so the sun's final rays fell upon the nail.

Gabriel? said she.

Bede? said she.

Cuthbert? Anthony? Godric? Does any Saint hear my plea?

My nail said naught.

Which direction shall protect us?

My nail said naught.

Did I do right?

Naught.

She let me go and busied herself in gathering up our meagre possessions.

Mam, I cry pardon, said I. *Mayhap I be not goode enough?*

She flew to me, held me tightly.

Never say it. You be special in ways you cannot comprehend, which be why the Angels and Saints—fickle though they be—dwell within thee. Never forget that.

We set out again. And though I saw naught in my nail, mayhap someone did guide our step, for next morn we reach't the sandy walls of Herthepoll...

56

...Friends, my first impression of that town was its drabness compared to Durham, but then the land slid away and I saw the sea. Upon its azure surface sparkled a million lights—enough candles to lift every last soul out of Purgatory in one soaring moment...

...Aye, friends, ye can laugh at mine words. After all, many of ye Mercers be able seamen long-accustomed to escorting thine fabrics across the Mediterranie. Oceans be naught but obstacles to commerce to you, tedious through familiarity. But to me then, who had never seen it, the vision was glorious. For Mam, too, as her trembling hand found mine.

Though as fugitives, we could not stand agog and drawing attention. Fortunately, attention was elsewhere that day, as it was Rogation. The streets teemed with banners, ringing hand-bells and raised crosses, as various parish guilds drove their evil spirits out from their own boroughs, and into those of their neighbours. Aggrieved accusations 'twixt guilds did fly— *Why hurl thine Imps into our street? Send them o'er to those bastards on Northgate!*—accusations which nevertheless set down a canny marker for Mam and me. We would need to remain hidden until the day after the following year's Rogation, for any villein away from his manor one year and a day was considered free by law.

Which was not an insignificant span. First, what of our lodgings? Behind one of Herthepoll's principal streets lay an alley of hovels constructed from beach timber. The parish guilds had made peace with these dens by agreeing to drive therein as one body their unwanted Rogation Devils. For there resided Herthepoll's vagabonds, and after much inquiry and fair portion of our purse, Mam secured us space within one.

This fetid alley had no given name, though many called it *Sturdy Row*—in mocking jest to its tottering shelters, but also the resident Sturdy Beggars who earned coin by deception. The soap-eaters who feigned frothing madness. Women who flash't their paps to some hot wight for to lure him into a dim cellar, where her gang awaited. In the construction we lived in, there aboded one man who had clubbed his own feet to jelly for to increase his gimp and thus the coin from those soft of heart.

But Sturdy Row was not all tricking beggars. Nay, many other honest folk lived there who despised those swindlers and chase't away the Sturdies if they came enquiring after a bowl of pottage or scrap of stockfish. Likewise, the Priests at St. Hilda's refused the Sturdy Beggars alms, which did not please the honest as much as you might think. For to clergy eyes, honest and Sturdy alike lived together upon Sturdy Row—mix't like tares and wheat—so that the honest wight was denied his fair portion of alms when the Priest, thinking only on Sturdy Row's reputation, drew no distinction 'twixt those deserving and underserving of charity.

As for Mam and me, the taint of Sturdy Row stuck to us also. Our money waxing scant, we sought work. First, we enquired with the villeins and freemen outside the walls, for we knew rustic ways best. But most treated us as vagabonds and sent us away. Those who did offer us day-labour, did so at even lower rates than Segerston. High costs at market prevented them from offering more, they said, though our visible hunger likely emboldened such claims.

Certain days, we lined up along the fishing docks, hoping the Steward would engage us to wash the stones of entrails and viscera—while also granting us chance to pluck up any morsels the gutting blades had miss't. Yet here, too, did we encounter reproach, not only from Fishingmen accusing us of theft, but from others on Sturdy Row vying to be waged. There was abundant work upon that slymy dock, but the Steward pick't fewer souls than needed, driving them harder to make the labour of many. Mam and me were unknowns in Herthepoll, thus the employment of us two aliens meant those who had lived their whole lives there did not get work. Bitterness ensued. One day, as I was tossing guts into the waters, a woman doing likewise put her hot gob to my ear as if speaking a secret.

Thy mam be a tall whore, she said. *Return whence you came, for we have no need of tall whores here.*

And I thought, why do you hate us so?
We be like thee?

133

Yet, stinking as the job was—to this day I cannot be in the same room as a lamprey—for the first tyme since Da died, light was creeping into Mam's eyes. Each day brought us closer to the hallowed day following next Rogation, when we would be free by law. As Purgatory eventually leads to Heaven, friends, so tribulation with fix't end be endurable. And Mam could endure. We both could. Thus, I let myself believe we would anon be free...

...But less than a month after coming to Herthepoll, as we were washing away the last fish guts from stones, a voice spoke upon the dock—

Alice Payne?

And Mam turned to see the Sheriff and his m—

57

—*Ach!*

My fukkit *head!* All of a sudden it pains me greatly. Friends, I cry pardon as I gulp my syrup bottle...

...*guhummm*...

...I see curiosity in many eyes as I take my medicine, and it strykes me that you, Mercers of Durham, might appreciate the origin of this concoction, for it concerns the Patron Saint of your guild—Godric of Finchale, whose feast we celebrate this day. Godric lived one hundred and five years, sixty of them in Finchale forest, then riddled with wolves and poison vypers. Yet he took that rough place and, using only sticks and turf,

134

built the Chapel of Saint John. From those humble beginnings now stands glorious Finchale Priory, and it be plain how perfectly match't Godric be as Patron of your guild. For while your luxurious mode of existence differs greatly from that hermit sleeping upon stones, ye Mercers be the same as Godric in fundamentals—both he and ye spin the greatest of miracles from the simplest of fabrics.

But it was not Godric who taught me the recipe of this medicinal syrup, for that wonderous hermit hath been dead two centuries. Nay, I learn't from a mortal man, the Physikian-scholar Lancaster Lambert who, while not capable of Saint Godric's marvels, was still able to provide socour to those in strife. Lord Lambert anon becomes an important character in our Wraith tale, as do his potions. Thus, I shall say how I came to know both...

58

...Earlier, I spoke of how Lancaster's childe Eric suffered from falling sickness. Well, afore the Lord began searching medical texts, he first sought cure from a more reasonable source—by means of Sainted Shrine. To Finchale Priory they went, a single mile from their castle. There, Eric touch't the tomb of Godric, for it be well known that a father had once brought Godric his dead boy in a sack, and that Saintly hermit had returned the lad to lyf. But for reasons unknown, Godric did not cure Eric, so Lancaster took his son about the country in search of a Holy Relic which might restore his health. In St. Bees, Eric saw the bracelet belonging to Saint Bega—that virgin who fled Ireland to escape a perverted Norseman—for touching it was known to cure the dropsical and swollen. In Buckston, alongside hundreds of groaning, woebegone souls with atrophied limbs and putrid wounds, he sup't the curing waters of Saint Ann's Well. At Peterborough cathedral, Lancaster and Eric witness't the Right Arm of Saint Oswald, which, though 800 years auld, remained as plump as the day it was severed. Surrounding each and every Shrine lay proofs of their power—the abandoned crutches cast aside by those no longer needing them. The false arms, legs, teeth and prevy parts fashioned from wax and left as testament by folk whose correspondent organs had been restored to goode use. Wax eyeballs by the thousand—so many they appeared as fallen snow—scattered by those blind no more; eyes watching Lancaster and Eric on their long pilgrimage, purchasing Shrine Badges and making large donations to the Church.

But alas, Eric continued to weaken.

Which be when Lancaster turned to medicine. He became known for his powerful apothecaries, though, lamentably, they did not save Eric. But Lancaster was a goode man, and after his son died, he used his skill to heal any sickened soul coming to his door. And come they did—for word noised about that Lord Lambert's medicines cured more reliably than some Saints. A constant line of the agonised wended to Lancaster's door. Folk with sweating sickness. With bad bellies and weeping buboes. With tooth worms and black gums and cataracts. Lancaster did what he could for all, as he did for me, when Pearl brought me to him to cure my paining head.

Eric had especially loved hearing Pearl play, as he had played for him while the boy died. We were thus assured a warm welcome, but as the Valet led us to the part of the castle which formed Lancaster's base of medical inquiry—rooms filled with simmering cauldrons, bushels of herbs, and bottles labelled in the man's scribeworthy hand—we heard voices in deep disagreement. Cutting vapours hung in the air as the Lord bickered with a Monk from Finchale Priory. And in one corner, a mother held her ailing childe.

Said the Monk, *Enticing the sick to thy door keeps them from true salvation at ours.*

How? replied Lancaster. *I use my God-given brain to help as best I can.*

They require not thy brain. You denigrate the Saints and clergy with thy "help".

Pearl said, *Be it denigration to place God above both?*

The Monk, who had not notice't our arrival, jounce't at Pearl. *And who are you, Lollard?*

The Monk went o'er to the cringing mother and childe.

Come away from this corrupting place, he said. *Finchale lies a mile from here, where thy lad shall touch Godric's tomb and be truly cured.*

Lassy, said Pearl. *Close thine ears to this man.*

Stow thy tongue, Lollard!

Monk, tell Godric he can tongue my crack, was Pearl's reply.

Wheezing most terrible, the boy droop't in his mother's arms. It was clear from her raggedness that she was a simple rustic, and terrified to be caught 'twixt a Monk, a Lord, and what seemed to be a foaming Lollard. Ever canny, Lancaster saw this, so flew to his potions and press't a small leather bottle into the mother's palm.

Four drops with water.

Leave it, said the Monk. *Godric will not hear thee with that witchery upon thy person.*

137

The woman put the bottle on the floor. As the Monk led them away, Lancaster turned to his shelves, clench't fists trembling. When he had composed himself, Pearl introduce't me as his apprentice who suffered from a squeezing skull. Lancaster pick't up the bottle he had offered the rustic mother, and the smell was fain powerful when he pulled the stopper. I ask't of the pungent liquid's origin.

Syrup of Devils-bit, said Lancaster. *Boiled down with a quantity of wort.*

Wort? said I. *Wort as in ale?*

Yes, though this syrup is of hundredfold potency and shall quell thy pain.

I took some upon my tongue. Almost immediately, my aching brain quietened. Lancaster saw my relief.

She had the cure in her hand, he said.

You tried, said I.

That will not help her boy. But no matter—Gleeman, take the bottle and there shall always be more here when you need it...

...Friends, I have just come from the Lamberts this day, hence this little bottle of Devils-bit reduction to sooth my paining head. For it hath been fain paining all throughout this bleak aside. The memory of the pale childe and his trembling mammy force't to give up their cure, well, it reminds me of Mam and myself near the end. An end, friends, we rapidly approach as we return to the Herthepoll Sheriff and his men, leading us away from the fishing docks...

59

...Gaol, then. Mam was taken away, and I was toss't into a cell filled with slyme and rats. Big rats. Tyme pass't, and I knew not if it was day or night. At intervals, I was hauled afore an inquisition. One of the Sheriff's men had a boil 'neath his eye, another stank of shite and enjoyed cupping my arse. Both demand answers to their questions, some of which I knew—

—*Be you free or villein?—*

—*What be thy family name?—*

—*Who thy Lord...?*

...But others I did not—

—*Who help't thee flee?—*

—*Were they dissident or Lollard?—*

—*Where be these agents now? SPEAK!...*

...This barrage they kept up 'til I fainted away with fear and hunger, for I was given naught but mouldy crusts to suck upon. I also suck't my thumbnail, to clean it of grime so that some Angel or Saint might appear to tell me how I might find Mam. Naught shewed itself. Endless days followed, and just as I thought I might die, I was pluck't from my pit and thrown into the back of wagon. Mam was there. Her lip was split, her eye purpled, her tunic torn about the breasts, but she was warm when I fell into her arms....

60

...Our flight from Segerston to Herthepoll had taken many nights. The return was completed in one. When the wagon doors opened, Thomas the Bailiff stood in the blinding morn sun with a queer look upon his pockmark't face—not anger, but some unsettled mixture of relief and sorrow the likes of which I have not seen since. The look was directed at me, and I almost wish't it *was* simple rage, for that at least I could understand. He step't forward to place his hand upon my head. I sense't other men standing each side of the wagon doors, beyond my perspective, and when Thomas nodded, Ralf Deepslough and his hairy sons took us up like grain sacks and carried us to the hallmote. The table was set 'neath the common green oak for the weather was temperate, but naught would be clement about the event for Mam and me.

At great length we were excoriated by the jurors and also many villeins, for our escape had added to their burdens. Even those who had previously shewed us compassion by their silence now jeered as the jury, led by Denis Daunt, amerce't Mam ten shillings—an enormous sum—and made her swear renewed fealty to thee, Sacrist, with the warning that if she fled again, she would be sent to Northgate gaol and tried by the Justices of the Peace.

That means flogging, said Denis. *Or years rotting in a dungeon.*

Throughout, Thomas the Bailiff said little. His eyes kept darting to mine, but I rebuff't them, for I had endured enough eyes upon me. All I wanted was to go hame and sleep. I sobbed sorely, but Mam could not comfort me because Thomas was now rousing himself to address her.

Alice Payne, said the Bailiff. *Do you accept the fines amerce't thee today?*

Mam said naught.

Very well, said the Bailiff. *I receive word of a cucking-stool erected in Durham, along the Wear at South Street. Continue in thy silence, and I shall see thee plunged for each penny you hast cost this manor. And if you be drownded, it matters naught to me. But what shall become of thy little one?*

Snivelling, I hid myself as best I could behind Mam.

So Alice, one final tyme—do you accept?

Friends, what mother could not...?

61

...We returned to our cottage. The back croft was thick with weeds and thatch-rot had grown apace. Mam gathered up the last twigs of deadwood to build a fyre, the kindling of which had barely caught afore Ralf leered in our doorway.

Alice, pleasing to see thee once again.

What do you want, Deepslough?

From the morrow onward, you harrow the Lord Sacrist's demesne.

Queer, but I thought Ralf said this without his usual mocking. Mayhap his conscience prick't? Then again, the Reeve knew well the first rule of animal hysbandry, that which the urban dock Steward of Herthepoll had not—namely, a beast flogged less can be flogged longer...

62

...So Herthepoll
became a dream as we laboured in long days of toil and aliena-
tion. Mam harrowed the demesne and ploughed the additional
wasted lands the Bailiff had pledged revive. This she did with
our sole remaining beast—the dray horse. After our escape,
this creature had emancipated itself from our glebe to spend its
woebegone days cropping the common field, and now returned
to us, it was even less inclined towards work.

My own work was to salvage our holdings. We had not yet
sown peas or vetches, and mix't in with the sprouting wheat
I could see much darnel growing. I thought of Father Bell's
denouncement of that weed, and the one-eyed Gleeman who
said consuming darnel granted vision to one's heart. *Strange*, he
had said of the taste. Well, I had had enough strangeness and
did not wish for more. I knew I needed to uproot the darnel
from our patch, but had no tyme for such an arduous task.
Besides my field duties, I had to tend the hearth, fetch water,
and cook our pottage—scant victual I took to Mam wherever
she was upon the Sacrist's demesne or wasted lands. Thin as
she was, she ate little and bade me take the larger portion.

Then after every Evensong, we prayed for Da and Christopher, for Sibyl and Robert. Mam carried me hame when I fell
asleep in church, and I possess one memory, vivid as a crack't
jewel in the crown of my tarnish't remembrance. The last tyme
I saw Mam alive...

63

...I was sleeping in the loft when the sound of water coax't me from slumber. Night was visible through our tattered thatch, and in befuddlement I thought the roof had given way 'neath a deluge of rain. This was not so. Peering down, I saw Mam afore the fyre, heating water in our pot. When it steamed, she used a pail to pour it into the barrel she had once used to brew ale. When it was tolerably filled, she brought a stool and stood upon it. Then, undoing tunic and kirtle and underclothes, she let them...

...fall...

...Ah, *friends*...

...I have begun this memory, but struggle to continue. Not for modesty, nay, but because I have never afore spoken of this night. Not even to Pearl. As Mam step't into the barrel, I saw every privation that had been wrought upon her...

...Saw shoulder bones near breaking through famish't flesh...

...Ribs and hip bones likewise...

...Bruised legs and arms from wrestling our dray horse...

...Feet blebbed and bloody...

...And a weeping wen low on her back that must hath screamed each tyme she bent to her labours...

...Lo, friends, this vision of my mother hath haunted me all my lyf—her brutalised flesh sinking down into that barrel. Sinking 'til the water closed o'er her and...

...Ah...

...and now we come to it. But afore we do, friends, recharge your glasses. Pour more ale, more wine. Drynke, everyone! You there, at that back table—drynke! Walter, Sacrist, Hugh de Tanfield—fill your cups and drynke.

Drynke deep, for what I tell next be not merry.

Nay, not merry at all...

64

...I did not see it happen. Mam was out harrowing the demesne, but when I took her pottage to those acres, she was not there. Instead, a small crowd had gathered—freemen, villein, and cottar alike, all speaking feverishly. When they saw me, they stowed their tongues. The same stricken look upon each face.

Where be Mam?

Walter, it was thy father Adelbert who spoke.

Lad...the horse.

He had been labouring nearby, so witness't all. Our bitter dray horse had refused to pull the harrow any further. Mam had heaved the bridle, and it had reared up but did not move forward. Adelbert said Mam then brok down screaming—in rage or despair he knew not—and began lashing the beast with a crop.

She was at the beast's back, said he. *It kick't out and caught her a blow to the skull.*

Where be she?! cried I.

Lad, she tumbled onto the harrow. Her arms became snared in the matrix, so when the horse bolted, she was carried off with it.

I saw parallel ruts of harrowed soil swerving away, the tracks marred by a large object dragged in its wake. The trail continued to the edge of the wasted land and into the fells...

...Thomas ordered a search, though it did not escape me how fewe of the village turned out, nor how quick they gave up. But me, I scoured the fells past dark, calling for Mam 'til I blew out my voice. Then I started again at first light, and did so for many days, though it was not I who eventually discovered the horse. Some cottar picking crow garlick found the thing—dead and half suck't into a bog, legs shattered. The wooden harrow lay mangled nearby, but of Mam there was no trace. To find her, I covered more fell than afore. I plunged into its grottos and fissures, ribboning my skin upon thorned gorse and bramble, each barb renting double.

First my flesh.

Then my heart...

...And now a third wounding here,

145

friends, as I recount the horror. For tyme cannot blunt those pricking spines. In dede, I swear they grow sharper with each passing year...

65

...Hugh de Tanfield, Cellarer—*former* Cellarer —when Mam was not found, you returned to Segerston to decide what must be done with our land, obligations, and *me*. It was another bright day, brisk with flies 'neath the common green oak. There, you enjoined the hallmote jurors to provide for me a guardian 'til I was of age to swear fealty to the Lord Sacrist. It was Stephen the Miller whom they chose to keep me, but Stephen kneeled in supplication to say his wyf was with childe, and with an additional belly soon to fill, he could ill afford to fill mine.

This was accepted by the jurors—at least, none mentioned the flour all knew he clandestinely sequestered from the sacks he milled. The jurors then called upon Neville Hille from the east part of the village. Neville was an even-natured villein, and well like't for it, so his rage fain jounce't all who heard it. He railed at the jurors o'er the twenty additional acres of wasted demesne that had recently been assigned to him, acres he could not manage alongside his other work owed to the Lord Sacrist. So, he raved, how might he also manage the lands which would one day become my inheritance? He could not even afford the entry fee! At great length did Neville erupt, and when, finally, he finish't, Denis Daunt spoke.

Neville, thy own son be of age. Can he not do more?

Neville dried his eyes with his tattered sleeve. *Shame on*

thee. Ye all know my lad be touch't, and cannot do as others his age can. The bald truth be if I must take another body 'neath my roof, he needs to be stronge and capable...not some stringy childe.

Cellarer, with powerful voice you informed Neville that his insubordination would see him amerce't, to which—and to the amazement of all—gentle Neville tore his empty purse from his belt and threw it upon the ground.

Take it from that.

Cellarer, I believe you were on the cusp of redressing this outburst, but then Ralf Deepslough whispered words into Thomas the Bailiff's ear, who then poured them into thy own. I imagine they had something to do with Neville Hille, that breaking one of Segerston's most unshakable villeins risk't tipping some collective balance. To thy credit, Cellarer, you heeded the warning and bade the jurors make their final pick— one Reginald Culpeper. Though this villein possess't goodly material wealth, the belligerent wight had also been entered many tymes into the court rolls for infractions. And true to form, though dew still clung to the grass, Reginald's speech was thick with Joan's ale. He also had plenty to say about taking me as his ward.

Stephen and Neville cry off this bairn for bellies to fill and acres to plough. Well, a fart I crack at bellies to fill and acres to plough! I say it plain—I shall never take that boy under my roof.

For what reason? ask't Denis Daunt.

For he be unnatural, like his mam. Because that cunte be still abroad somewhere.

Culpeper, that be no reason.

I disagree. Where she be? If she lives, why hath she not returned? And if she be dead, that goes all the worse, for she died without shrift or housel and be now a ghost bent upon vengeance.

Reginald poynted out beyond the fields, towards the vast fells.

Out there, her soul be trap't inside a walking corpse...

Then he poynted at me.

...And when she returns for her boy—and she will—calamity befalls us all.

Segerston's rustics moved away from raving Reginald. But they were not fearful *of* him, rather of what he said. Thomas, though, had indulged enough. Mindful of the warning you, Cellarer, had given him last tyme you were there, the Bailiff was determined to shew his mettle. He slammed his fist down hard upon the table to stow Reginald's tongue, then spoke in firm tones of command.

I let this bickering go on, said he, *in hopes it would lead to a decision regarding the childe. But I see now that was folly. Jurors, have ye made a decision?*

Denis Daunt look't at his fellows, then back to Thomas.

Nay.

Then it is for me to settle things.

Straightening to full height, the Bailiff took a deep breath.

I shall take the Payne boy, he said.

Murmurs through the crowd, for this was a queer turn. Hugh—Cellarer—thy voice shook with anger.

Bailiff, you said, *custom dictates only a villein shall take as his charge an orphaned villein. This you surely know.*

But—

But naught. As Bailiff, you follow custom.

Thomas hung his head and cried pardon. But Hugh, you cared naught for pardons as you glared out upon the gathered villagers.

Reeve, you said. *Reeve, shew thyself.*

The crowd that had parted from Reginald now isolated Ralf. For the first tyme, I saw the man afeard.

Stand beside the boy, you said, Cellarer.

When Ralf had done so, you continued.

Deepslough be thy name?

Aye, Cellarer.

And thy wyf?

Joan, sir. Joan Deep—

Her betrothed appellation I can deduce for myself.

Cry pardon, sir.

Joan is past childe bearing?

Ralf's eyes sought out his wyf, who look't as stricken as her hysband.

Sir, we hope God shall bless us once more.

You called for Joan to approach. As you appraised her, Joan's hands shielded herself as if she stood naked afore all.

Reeve, if you think this one gives thee another bairn, you are a simpleton.

Aye, sir.

Thomas step't forward. Mayhap he was thinking of the eternal damnation awaiting if he rejected God and allowed Segerston to fail. Cellarer, you saw this too, so allowed the Bailiff to address Ralf Deepslough himself.

But what of thine actual children? ask't Thomas. *You hast sons of age?*

Three, Bailiff. Philip, Theobald, and Ber—

In body and mind, are they able?

Aye.

Well, said Thomas. *Three young men to work thine holdings and the Lord Sacrist's demesne. How fortunate. And to be Reeve as thine ancestors were afore you, so I am told. A legacy of stronge men with*

149

stronge heads upon stronge shoulders. Men not easily swayed by hysterics, Reeve?

Ralf said naught, for he had been led into a trap; one the stronge head upon his stronge shoulders was not stronge enough to think on means of escaping.

Thus, Deepslough, continued the Bailiff, *by thy own admission, you hast shewed thyself master of the obstacles befalling Stephen, Neville and Reginald. And on top of all—you are this year's Reeve. A Deepslough Reeve at that. You are not a false Reeve, are you? One who abuses his station by helping his idle mates shirk their responsibilities to their Lord?*

Nay, said Ralf.

You do not fiddle thine tallysticks at the Lord's expense? Say I nosed about thine outhouses, I would not find stolen bushels from last year's reap?

Some rustics exchange nervous looks. Clearly, the Bailiff had more about him than they thought.

Never, said Ralf, pale now.

That gladdens me, for I would see such a man flogged. As reward for thy goodness—take this childe under thy roof. Tend his lands 'til he be of age. Jurors, do ye object?

Denis Daunt look't to his jurors. He did not look to Ralf.

Nay, said Denis.

Thomas paused. Cellarer, I wonder if thee sense't trepidation in the Bailiff? Sadness, even? I did, but in a moment his authority returned.

Clerk, said Thomas. *Record Ralf Deepslough as the boy's guardian.*

As the Clerk shook off his quill, Ralf stared down at me with throbbing fury.

Bailiff, I thank thee for this honour...

...So off I went to live
with Ralf Deepslough, a man now long dead who nevertheless continues to ambush me when I least expect. Friends, in
Cestria not a week ago, I heard a song about the night the Fell
Wraith struck Segerston. I had never heard it afore, so listened
rapt 'til the young singer's last note. When I ask't where he
had learned it, he said it was his own composition. A lad
barely twenty years auld! Proof, surely, the Wraith still dances
through Durham's moonlighted lands and minds. Allow me
to play it. The tune be a mournful one—

> *Brok-Armed Annie jigged that night,*
> *Putrid face full shining bright,*
> *Cast from gibbous Moon above*
> *Lonely Segerston, filled whereof,*
> *With blackened crop and blacker fear,*
> *As the Wraith drew ever near,*
> *Dancing 'twixt their dwellings dim,*
> *She spun and shook her fetid limbs,*
> *'Til anon her froliks came,*
> *To the Reeve's own very hame,*
> *Inside, there shivered many folk,*
> *Who knew the Wraith they had provok't,*
> *And thus afeared their days soon end,*
> *By she whom they did grave offend,*
> *So in turn shall their graves reach not,*
> *Severed from their Lord, forgot,*
> *Their souls lock't in foul flesh corrupt,*

Chewed by wormes and fluids sup't,
Forever more in Death's ensnare,
Until that final trumpet blare,
Then gulp't down by the mouth of Hell,
Where flames and fangs and fiends do dwell,
In gallimaufrous agony,
Writhing for eternity,
Then, anon, her spree began,
Butchering woman, childe, and man,
The rustics there knew they would die,
'Til—hark!—was raised the hue and cry!
Yet not the village roused anon,
For there was stood but only one—
Against the dead, the Reeve alive,
Turning in his hand a scythe,
To fight the fiend unconsecrated,
And battled thus, 'til fiend abated,
Mortal wounded, Reeve expired,
As the Wraith then quench't her ire,
Towards the Manor House she fled,
To burn it up and render dead,
All the souls that hid within,
Who to the last perish't in sin,
Yet for some others, it was reprieve,
His lyf for theirs did give the Reeve...

...Though
his name be not sung direct, it shivers me Ralf Deepslough
lives on in such songs. Not that I want the man's memory to
rot faster than his flesh—of *course* not! Only the verse muddles
truth, for it was *not* the Reeve who wielded the scythe that

bloody night. Nay, it was another. But we shall come to that
anon! My poynte be, in rustic retellings of the Fell Wraith these
long years, Ralf Deepslough hath become a hero. This saddens
me, for the valiant Ralf in the lad's song be not the Ralf I knew...

67

...Now he was responsible for their upkeep, Ralf put me to
work upon my father's holdings. As ye might imagine, they
were in grave disarray. The darnel that had begun sprouting afore Mam died now rioted through our wheat. I wish't
uproot them, but Ralf demanded so many other things be
righted first—ditches dug, fences fastened, walls wattled. The
roof thatch now held more vermin than straws, so Ralf bade
me strip it—a task even ye, Mercers, who enjoy urban lives
'neath slate rooves, must see be a job for a gang of men, not a
single boy still shy his eleventh year. Each fist of straw I tugged
away revealed my auld hame below, the place I had once lived
happily. Now it was empty of objects—for our furniture and
chattels had gone to thee, Sacrist, and to Father Bell also.

And empty of people, too.

At nights, fain weary, I stumbled back to Deepsloughs'. Ralf
and his family would oftentymes be sat about the fyre, eating
barley stew with salt pork. Joan would see my gob flood at
the smell and fill a bowl for me, but afore giving it, would ask
for the secret to Mam's ale. When I said again there was no
secret, she handed the bowl to Ralf or one of her boys to shovel
into their gobs. Nor was I permitted to sleep in the warm loft
with them. Instead, after mine toils, I climbed the ladder to
the opposite loft—a tiny, treacherous perch of unstable boards

where naught was kept, for aught heavier than myself was likely to fall through. In dede, on cold nights, I was afeard mine shiverings would be enough to send me crashing to my death.

Still, this eyrie was a decent roost from which to observe. Most evenings, I put my eye to cracks 'twixt the loose loft lumbers and watch't the village supping Joan's tedious brew. Dark words did the rustics mutter about dwindling stores and scant coin, 'til eventually the less stoic wights began weeping into their ale at the prospect of the failed harvest and subsequent destitution. Villeins raged at the additional demesne the Bailiff now bade them work, while freemen grutch't o'er the Mercer apprenticeship, for events there had taken a queer turn. George Goodsell slop't ale across the table and moaned that the Bailiff had not chosen his son, but instead it was Adelbert Attwell's lad now in Durham with Duncan Harpour. Of all the village freeman, George possess't the most means, while Adelbert was poorer than some villeins, so how come *his* boy, Walter, had got the nod? Nay, said George, something fukkit *slippery* goes on.

Throughout this nightly bitterness, Joan did her best as Taverness. She jape't and jangled while topping up the ale, asking hopefully of its flavour. *Aye, Joan,* all would say. *Aye, it be fine,* but when she turned away, sour faces did they pull. Joan often caught sight of their scorn, smiling in the pretence she had not...

68

...One night, after all drynkers had gone hame, I was shivering in my loft when Osbert the Valet rap't upon the door. Peeping down through the cracks, it warmed my nithered heart to see Ralf quail at the man's arrival.

Sir? cringed the Reeve.

The Payne childe, said Osbert. *Where be he?*

Ralf's dread deepened. Had news of my mistreatment found Thomas' ear?

Sleeping, sir. In the loft sleeping.

Fetch him.

Aye, sir.

Ralf called my name but I did not respond. Let the bastard sweat. Anon, Ralf climbed the ladder, so I feigned sleep, forcing him to rouse me not as usual, with painful jabs and curses, but a false-gentleness that inwardly must hath sickened him.

Come back to us, lambkin. A man wishes see thee.

Pretending befuddlement, I opened mine eyes. From below, Osbert would not be privy to Ralf's evil expression, which spoke contra to his tender tongue—*keep thy fukkit gob shut, boy, or I shall flay thee alive.*

I came down. There was a gimp in my walk from where Ralf's eldest, Philip had kick't me days prior. Ralf telt Osbert I had fallen when foolishly trying to haul more fyrewood than mine feeble arms could carry.

I tell him he be o'er young for adult labours, said Ralf. *But does he hear it?*

Master wishes speak with the childe in the manor, said Osbert.

Pray tell, upon what subject? ask't Joan, then malting grain by the fyre.

Ignoring her, Osbert march't me out into the night. In darkness upon the village edge, the manor house took on grand and ominous dimension. Hellfyre light dripp't from the gaps in the boarded windows, and my head filled with every rumour

I had heard about goings-on in that place. At the backdoor, Osbert turned an iron key and shoved me inside. The only other stone building I had ever entered was the parish church, but where that place was lofted and grand, the manor was close. Suffocating. Much furniture lay splintered upon the flagstones, and there was a comingled smell of shite and spew. Osbert poynted to a doorway.

In there, said he. *Master awaits.*

The Valet went upstairs afore I could ask him what Thomas wanted of me. I crept to the door, listening hard, when a voice spoke from within.

The frame is swollen. Muscle it.

It opened with a grim shriek but Thomas did not wince at the sound. He was lolling in a chair so near the fyre it was a wonder he and it both were not one pile of ashes. Shadows giddied o'er the Bailiff's visage, pitted and pock't like some blighted turnip.

Lad, he said thickly. *Laaaaaddddddddy.*

Though he now made effort to shew elsewise in his public Bailiff dealings, privately the drynk still ruled him. Thomas reach't for the leather bottle by his chair, but it was empty.

Osbert! he bellowed. *More wine!*

Osbert did not stir.

Base churl, muttered the Bailiff, exiting the room and leaving me alone.

I look't about mine surroundings. In the middle of the room was a long table for feasting guests, but as nobody had dined at the manor since Thomas' arrival, it rioted with one man's mess. Congealed bowls of stewed vegetables—remember, he was forbidden meat—and dozens of empty cups and bottles. Amid this wreckage lay several wood-bound books. I had never seen a book. One was the Bible, open at Malachi. And though it was written in Latin, thanks to thine lessons, Walter, I could read it still—*Ecce enim dies veniet succensa quasi caminus et erunt omnes superbi et omnes facientes impietatem stipula et inflammabit eos dies...*

...a verse, friends, that I shall not translate directly for risk of being flayed as a Lollard, so say only it refers to the arrival of a day that shall burn like an oven, scorching away the wicked and the proud like the stubble of a reap't field...

...Scattered 'twixt these books and bowls were curls of paper—a gauzy material compared to the Bible's sturdy parchment—all covered in writing. Thomas seemed to be composing missives to several associates, either asking for money or begging additional grace in its repayment. Clearly, they were not easy words for him to write because there was much slashing of ink, and several blackened drafts in the hearth. Yet I now quoth one composition much further advance't.

To myn Fader Duncan Harpour, greetings from hys Sone Thomas Harpour. I have ben stationed Bailiff ov Segerston Manere some months an it doth seeme alle goeth welle apace. Ther wer Issues in neede ov resolve in this Playce, as ther wyll allus be thus with Comon Rustics, for they possess Natural Ignorance. But I have met this Challynge with Stern Hart. These Rustics learnt myn weyes an Respeckt me for them an now alle be welle. The Harvest schall be secure an Bountyfull an I shoulde wish Thee noe this. Prithee my Mother be welle. I hold her in myn Prayers trewly as I do Thee, Fader. I bese—

—*You are lettered?* said Thomas, standing in the doorway with a fresh bottle in fist.

The smile touching his wine-black lips quickly became a grimace when he saw what I was reading. Plucking up the letter, he stuff't it in his purse and fell back into his chair. The claret spill't down his surcoat as he drank. Sable, sanguineous drops. Sighing, he ask't who had taught me to read.

My friend Walter Attwell, I replied. *He learns at the grammar school.*

Amicum tuum? Itane?

Ita.

The Bailiff's smile returned.

Walter Attwell...son of the freeman Adelbert? A bright boy. I recommended him to my father, who is fain pleased with the lad.

Walter's mind be sharp.

It was if he did not hear me.

They say you are a goodly singer.

I know not.

Sing for me?

But I was o'er shy. Thomas shewed his teeth, dim from wine and tooth worms.

I bring thee here as respite from the Reeve. Prithee, return the favour.

So I found mine culls, and sang—

> *You be loved*
> *Hear my plea*
> *You be loved*
> *You be me*
> *'Til we meet*
> *Once again*
> *In my love*
> *Never end...*

...A tear trembled upon the Bailiff's closed lashes. When my song ended, he drank off his cup.

Whose song is that?

Mam sang it to me.

Her body hath still to be found?

I search't everywhere, Bailiff. 'Neath every gorse and heather, but she was not there.

I imagine she is never far from thine thoughts?

And dreams.

His bleared eyes sharpened. *Tell them to me.*

It was an error to speak of mine dreamings. They were private to me, and I did not then understand their meaning. I telt Thomas I always dreamt of Mam the same way—that final night I saw her, sinking naked into her auld ale barrel. In the dreams, I step upon the stool to look down into the water as dark and vast as the sea at Herthepoll. Mam floats deep below. I reach my hand 'neath the surface to pull her up, but she grabs me and hauls me down with her. Then I wake.

Thomas listened with troubled countenance. I thought he might demand more particulars—or declare me mad—but he did neither.

Dreaming is a queer business, said he.

Aye, Bailiff.

Sing her song again.

So I did, more surely than the first tyme.

A pretty ditty, said he when I finish't. *But now thy family is gone, do you believe the sentiment? Can one endure without another to love them?*

Friends, what childe could answer such a question? Thomas realised this anon.

Does it trouble thee, said he, *that thy mother died without shrift or housel? .*

It...it does, Bailiff.

Thomas.

Thomas, it troubles me greatly.

More wine went down his throat.

I am the mirour of thy mammy, said he. *For I was given final shrift and housel, yet did not die. God pluck't me from Death. I was thy age.*

I be...I be glad of that, Thomas.

I do not know if I am. My soul is split—one youthful part sent into Purgatory that day, the other growing spongy and rotted afore thee here now.

Again, I could not reply to such queer words.

I have brothers, Thomas continued. *Do you know of them?*

One be a Monk in the Priory. The other a Man of Law.

He smiled like a Tutor to his best student.

*Gossip never fails. But what you say is true—my younger siblings hoard victory like villeins hoard dung, and all who see them cannot but see me as failure in relation. Yet they do not consider mine brothers have made their names with their souls intact. How could I do likewise, with only half my animus? The half suffering in Purgatory, its agony robs me of all peace. All sleep. And this—*he beat weakly at his chest—*this heart is cleaved likewise. Only half alive. Or already half dead.*

Friends, to this day I know not why the following escape't my gob.

Though it be cleaved, Thomas, thy heart can still see.

The Bailiff cock't his head. *Childe?*

People fear that—seeing what their heart sees.

He frowned.

Did the Attwell boy also teach thee that?

Nay. A Gleeman.

A Gleeman? That makes sense. Like crows do, such wandering men pluck up shiny ideas without knowing their meaning.

Thomas bade me sit upon his knee. His sickly ruin smelt strongly of fermentation, and his flesh had an organ-sick yellowness not attributable to the fyrelight playing across his mottled face. Even the whites of his eyes were mealy brown as he watch't me.

You think me some hideous Goblin?

Nay, sir.

Well, I think it of myself. But there is one part of me that is champion of all others—mine ears. For though they think I do not, I hear freemen moaning about empty purses. Cottars demanding higher wages. Villeins grutching o'er labour obligations. I hear all, lad, and it shews the flaw in rustic thinking. Do you know the flaw of which I speak?

His leg jounce't me up and down, up and down.

I do not, Thomas.

They believe themselves the only ones caged by fate. But we are all birthed into our private cells, without reprieve or escape. We take it with us...wherever we go.

He press't his greasy, pitted cheek to mine.

Sing...once again...

As I did, he stroke't my hair, and continued doing so long after my song ended. When eventually his hand droop't, I thought the wine had lulled him to slumber. But then he whispered into my ear.

It was the freeman...Adelbert Attwell.

Sir?

So I would send his boy as apprentice...

...he came to me and

said...

        ...You would be found...

               ...In Herthepoll...

...Friends, I ask't Thomas to repeat his words, but the wine really did take him then. The cup slip't from his fingers, and when he commence't snoring, I slid likewise from his lap and left that place...

69

    ...More fevered talk at the head table! Walter, I believe you once more wish call the Guards! But wait, I do not defame thee. Mayhap, it was simple error? Mayhap one day you mentioned to thy father our talk at the deer park wall—of Mam's connection to Herthepoll—as an unthinking childe might any morsel, and it was *Adelbert* who saw it to be the one thing he might offer Thomas that richer freemen could not. Or mayhap, when thy da saw the Bailiff's desperation to get Mam back afore the Cellarer found out, he coax't Herthepoll from thine lips so gently you did not notice thy betrayal? Walter, all I know be that, weighing the apprenticeship against what it would cost Mam and me, never would you offer that knowledge wittingly.

  Be that true, Walter...?

        ...Wal—

...Walter, I understand! You need not scream! Aye, *fetch* the Guards if you wish, but afore you do, *think on*, sir. Think on thy father who, at this very moment, languishes in Kepier Hospital. Last tyme I saw him, the Nuns had tied his hands for he had tried *clawing out his own eyes.* And laughing as he did so—always laughing, laughing, laughing.

But laughing at *what*, Walter?

And *why?*

And while you think on that, think also on thy mam, Mabel, who died suddenly without shrift or housel, and be thus forbidden entrance to Purgatory. Walter—*you shall never meet thy mother in Heaven!* Do you not wish learn who robbed thee of that? Many folk say it was the Fell Wraith, aye, but you know there be rumours of another killer.

That it was thy own *father* who did it...

...Walter, I see you hast heard those gossips also. Well, I know the truth of it and you do not. For when Mabel died, you were in Durham, safe 'neath Duncan Harpour's roof, and so did not witness things as I did. So, shall you hast me hauled off to gaol, or shall you hear the end? And to sweeten the thing further, here be my offer—let me finish my tale, and if you *still* be unsatisfied, you can hang me in the market squ—

...Aye, Walter, I hear thee plain, for you roar like a Woodwose! Aye, you can do that also! Boil me in oil and mount my head on a spyke! So, Walter, we have an accord? As one auld friend to another...

...Thank
thee. Then I shall continue. There be not much left to tell...

70

...Though talk of the Woodwose reminds me of one thread still
a-dangle. Earlier, I promise't you that afore this night ended, I
would sate your curiosity o'er the Woodwose who was really
a man. Well, the night grows long and this be as goode a tyme
as any.

In truth, I be not long in knowing the tale myself. I was
performing at a tourney in celebration of the feast of Saint
Lawrence. Much jousting and gaiety was there, and many stripe
of Balladeer, Fabulator, and Tumbler. Mummers, too, with one
in particular taking my eye, for unlike his mates, this Mummer
was not disguised in usual fashion as stag or boar, Imp or
Goblin. Nay, he was straggled in fur, with sharpened bones
attach't to his fingers, and a pair of wooden stilts looming him
twice the height of a regular man.

Friends, this Mummer was a Woodwose.

Upon his appearance, naturally did I find myself telling my
own audience of my Woodwose experience. I felt queer doing
so, however, for these past twenty years, it had always been
Pearl who telt of that day. But Pearl was dead, and I had inherited the story along with his psaltery. Still, strange as it was, I
also felt gratitude. *Think on the tale*, Pearl had said behind the
boulder when I had wanted to flee. *Think on the tale you shall
one day tell of this.* And now that day had arrived.

My departed friend felt close to me then.

At the tourney, I telt of how Pearl and I had met the

fearsome beast. My audience gasp't at my description of the cave carvings, cross't themselves during our flight through the forest, and laugh't in amazement to discover the creature was not Woodwose, but *human*. I accepted the applause and whatever coin fell into my hat, and was preparing to move on when an auld man approach't. I had notice't this fellow in the crowd—heavily gimp't in the leg and stoop't o'er a walking staff that would not look amiss in the gnarled hand of the great sage Merlinus.

Greetings, Gleeman, said he. *My name is Sir Ivo Longspur. I am a Knight, now retired, who fought many battles and killed those deserving it.*

Longspur then ask't a question none whom had previously heard the Woodwose tale had ever ask't.

The patterns in the cave, did they look like this?

He pulled a dagger from the sheath upon his belt. Along the steel blade were engraved the same hart-tongue ferns I had last seen scratch't inside that lair. Feeling myself once again drifting into the depths of the design, I accepted the Knight's invitation to accompany him back to his cottage, so that he might tell a tale of his own...

...Sitting afore his hearth, drynking his magnificent wine—again, friends, I implore you to imbibe!— the Knight named Longspur spoke of his youth. The third son of a noble house whose eldest brother inherited all land and titles, Longspur made his way as do many minor sons of nobility—by becoming an errant Knight. In 1380, he joined the retinue of the Duke of Gloucester, then preparing an army in support of John the Conqueror's claim to the Breton throne. In July of that year, Gloucester ferried five thousand men—Longspur among them—o'er to Calais, and set about a campaign of annihilation. With the armies of the Duke of Burgundy harrying his heels, Gloucester scythed through France in a devastating chevauchée lasting into autumn. The English razed everything in their path, leaving naught but death and black plumes of funeral smoke to grief the horizon.

Finding new pleasure in auld carnage, Longspur lingered long in the telling of this. Thus, it was some tyme afore he came to the Blacksmith boy.

He was one of scores of rustic Smiths recruited from Gloucester's many estates, and brought to France. But word of this lad soon noised 'twixt the Knights, for his skill elevated his work o'er his Blacksmith peers, just as his physikal height elevated his head o'er theirs. It was due to this extreme tallness that all called him *Legumen*. His true name, said retired Sir Longspur, had long since fallen from memory, but what he *did* recall was the unparalleled nature of the lad's smithing. Greave and gauntlet, poleyn and pauldron—each piece forged true, their every contour exquisite. His blades, too, were sharpest of all, and along their whetted edges the young Smith engraved the most intricate motifs.

Like hart-tongue ferns, said the auld Knight, touching the dagger on his belt.

During Gloucester's long rape through France, Longspur returned to Legumen many tymes for adjustment and mending of his equipment. And though he was a highborn Knight and the lad a lowly rustic, Longspur confess't they developed a simulacrum of friendship.

And from our speaking, I saw warring did not suit him.

The slaughter of French rustics too slow in seeking the safety of city walls did chew his mind, said Longspur, and

166

a great dejection sank onto the boy. But it was not for Sir Longspur to raise him up. This was *war*. The concerns of a Blacksmith ought not trouble a warrior upon enemy land, especially come Gloucester's inept siege of Nantes in October 1380, which was when the true butchery began. French archers atop the city's impenetrable walls spill't much English blood, as did the wicked night raids—French assassins creeping into camp to murder the billeted invaders. Then came brutal winter and pestilence broke out. In early 1381, Gloucester fled the siege and what remained of his ragged army retreated a hundred miles north to Brittany, where hope of boats back to England awaited. Burgundy's men hounded them at every step, snatching any Englishman who fell behind. Longspur heard rumours the French did terrible things to those they caught— cut out their tongues and let them return to their ranks in order to sow greater terror there. But the Knight could not vouchsafe the truth, for he had his own lyf to save. And in doing so, Longspur forgot Legumen...

...But in the years following, the lad came to his mind whenever a fellow Knight at some tourney would comment upon his engraved dagger. Longspur then dallied in thoughts of finding Legumen, but there were always more jousts. More wars to fight. The auld Knight telt me of the throats he went on to open in Flanders, then Prussia, where pagans infest the forests of that place. Several tempestuous affairs he also conducted, including with the youngest daughter of the Baron of Kydyminster, though, muttered Longspur, the less spoken of *that* the better.

In such intrigues, said he, *twenty and more years went by.*

Until a tourney held by a Lord known for the succulence of

his venison. While there, Longspur learn't of a foe he had yet to face—the Woodwose. Immediately, he pledged to dispatch this creature and so curry favour with the Lord, for surely the nobleman did not wish such a Fiend loose amongst his deer?

Deep into the forest he went, eventually finding the creature's lair. Whispering a prayer to Saint George, he drew his sword and charged, but the cave was empty. Still, though the Knight did not engage in battle, he reeled as if struck a mighty blow.

The cave walls, said I.

The patterning, replied auld Longspur.

He said he then heard movement in the trees and the giant figure shambled into view. It was him. Legumen. The Knight spoke his name and when Legumen turned, Longspur saw him fully for the first tyme in decades. His body cake't in impenetrable filth. The rancid animal furs. The fleas crawling about his gauntness. But *something*, said Longspur, *something* stirred in his eyes. Some flickering remembrance. An ember of humanity...

Then he screamed, said the Knight. *And did so in such anguish that I, who have slewn more men than I can number, was chilled to the marrow.*

I heard it too, said I. *It shall ring in mine ears evermore.*

The auld Knight shook his head as if to rid it of the memory. *Battle can deform a man's mind as easily as his flesh. Seeing Legumen as the Woodwose, I knew his lyf after Nantes had been thus, and that he was beyond saving. So I left him alone.*

Longspur then went to the Venison Lord and relayed the sorry tale entire. When he was done, the Lord spoke.

And you came close to dispatching the creature?

Fain close.

The Lord's lips press't white. Longspur's first thought
was the man was shock't to hear such a sad, strange creature
encroach't upon his lands. Thus, the Knight sought to calm the
nobleman, which was when those lips twisted into a smirk.

Sir Knight, I have long known this wretch abides in mine forests.
Now Longspur was the one shock't.

Yet you did not help him?
And this Lord—known for his venison, boundless generosity, and goode works of charity—this Lord laugh't himself
to tears.

Help him? said he. *Since that shaggy thing took up residence, no
man dare poach my famous deer. The fiend be the finest Gamekeeper
in the land—and he works gratis!*

Fiend? said the Knight. *He is a man, sir.*
Not any longer.
My Lord?
He is more use as a Woodwose than a man...

...Friends,
I gave thanks for the wine and left Longspur's hame with a
leaden heart. For all I could think was, if God made the Blacksmith a Man...

...It was Man made him a Woodwose...

71

...Friends, does Legumen's story move you? Have ye ever
pondered how forces greater than the poor man sweep his lyf
from him? How the debts of the rich be paid by his destitute

cousin? If not, ye should. For these questions cut to marrow of what happened in Segerston when the Fell Wraith came to that place.

Mercers?

Sacrist?

Hugh de Tanfield?

Walter?

Have such considerations ever darkened your minds...?

...Not a one here speaks? Be ye in goode spirits? In truth, ye all look fain queasy—mayhap something ye ate? Still, I assumed men of your rank capable of the metaphysiks of acquisition. But no matter, for I shall *shew* you all what I mean as we return to Segerston...

72

...and the hectic reaping months fast approaching. The strain upon the village was unbearable, and grievance flowed freely. Thus, after Mass, Father Bell would describe to us the damnation we risk't by our continued dis-agreement and embitterment with our rustic lots. Upon his altar, the Priest gnash't his teeth.

God grows so angry that he shall smite you down anon. It hath happened afore, and not so long ago. I speak of the Great Pestilence. Your ancestors also refused their God-given fates, so God scoured them from the World.

Father Bell got onto his knees.

Now ye all repeat their error! Ye allow tares to riot amid the wheat. So I beg you, uproot those evil weeds! Uproot those dissatisfactions and free your hearts from grievance, afore ye are denied salvation for all tyme!

Yet tyme would be shortest of all for Father Bell. Come late July, his anguish o'er our souls won out against his mortal body, and he collapse't in church, clutching his heart. Hurridly, the Sexton gave the Priest shrift and housel, allowing him to die a goode death right there 'neath the south window. The one with the fresh lead...

...But Father Bell's sacrifice was not in vain. I had heard his words, and would no longer allow grievance to boil within my own heart. Thus, I awoke early and went to my father's lands and completed the task I had hitherto avoided—I uprooted the darnel from the wheat. It took days, for the weeding was long o'erdue, but when it was finally done, I went to Joan and cried pardon for my truculence. They had taken me 'neath their roof, and I had been ungrateful. To make amends, I would shew her Mam's brewing method. And it was true—there *was* no secret. Just care, attention...and the careful selection of grain. Joan watch't as I did as Mam had done. I malted and mash't. Cooled the wort ahead of fermentation. Scrape't away the scum. Joan was fain pleased as I taught her these things. And *I* was pleased when, a week later, she removed the lid of her barrel and filled a cup with Mam's ale. Joan drank it off, declaring it the best she had ever sup't. And her triumph was my own, for she then enjoined me to brew a fresh barrel every week.

Which I did, friends, and gladly...

73

...In the middle of
August, Denis Daunt step't out of Joan's tavern to make water.
A minute later, we heard him scream. Peering through my
crack in the loft, I saw Denis crash in and shut the door tight,
piss a-dribble down his leg.

South field, gasp't he. *Far edge.*

What be you blethering about? ask't Ralf.

A figure.

A figure? sneered the Reeve.

A woman, said Denis. *Moving queerly...dancing.*

Said Joan, *Since when does a woman make you scream like
a bairn?*

The other drynkers laugh't. Denis did not.

No normal woman...her jig was terrible. Loose arms flopping like...

Like what, man? ask't Stephen the Miller.

Like they were brok.

At this, Denis' mocking friends hush't.

She swayed, continued Denis. *Swayed to music I could not
hear...then she turned to me—merciful God in Heaven—she turned
and her fukkit face was all gore and—*

And you hast sup't o'er much ale! bellowed Ralf in jovial
fashion. But I was attuned to the man's bellowing by then, and
this rang with false courage.

Stephen the Miller ask't, *You saw this woman's face?*

Dear God, I wish I had not.

Who was she?

Denis Daunt poynted up at my loft.

The boy's mother, Alice Payne...

74

...

...Aye, so there it be...

...The Fell Wraith of innumerable tales and songs—the monster they say sways across the land to this day—she be my own mam.

And though I was forbidden leaving my loft, I flew down the ladder and into the night. Denis had seen her scant minutes prior, but the south field look't empty. The wheat was taller than I was then, so mayhap she hid inside? Calling her, I ran into the stalks 'til I arrived at the field's far edge, but she was not there. Instead, I saw a flattened circle of wheat much rotted...

75

...Word of the sighting noised quickly about Segerston. Later that same week, the Wraith must hath dance't through several dozen more acres for they, too, turned rotted. Next, folks' oxen sickened, their hen eggs filled with slyme and deformed, eyeless chicks. The cows on the common pasture filled milk pails with lumps of bobbing pus. Their owners fed bless't salt and Holy water to their beasts, and paid the Sexton to copy onto parchment the opening of Saint John's Gospel— *Verbum caro factum est*—which they tied to the shrivelled udders, but still the cows ailed. And with this ailing, came questions.

Was this merely some common blight which had struck their crops?

Their cattle sick due to insufficient fodder from near-empty stores...?

...Or was it the *Wraith?* The ghost they said was Alice Payne...?

...No answer was found, and soon hundreds of acres were naught but fly-blown slop. The more the village fretted, the more folk claimed to hath seen her—a figure in the distance, a twilit flitting, a shadow in the corner of the eye. Alice Payne, and no mistake, for who else *could* it be? As Reginald Culpeper had foreseen—her sudden death had lock't her unshriven soul inside her corpse. From Alice's boy, folk now kept their distance. Folk who had hitherto either ignored me, or made me subject of their scorn.

Now the malignant and indifferent alike quake't at my approach.

Now I was the Son of the Ghost...

...During the evenings, rustics of every stripe crowded into Joan's tavern—now festooned with Mare Stones to ward off evil—and discussed what might be done. It made Joan's the most success-ful business in Segerston, and I was turning out three barrels of ale a week. Even those who had previously not been much for drynk were now found with cup in hand. In dede, Walter, thy father Adelbert was an extreme case. Stowed in one corner, he poured the stuff ceaselessly down his gullet, fondling rosaries and muttering Paternosters, as the rest of the village

fell to rancour. Nobody agreed upon the meaning of Alice
Payne's ghost, nor what might be done about her. Night after
night, I listened to their ale-sodden voices below my loft.

*Father Bell warned this would happen—God sends this Wraith
to smite us.*

*Then we smite the Wraith! Do it like the auld days—find her lair,
cut off her head and put it by her cunte, then bury her likewise. That
hath been the way since tyme out of mind.*

That does not sound like a Christian method, Roland.

Nay, John, but it be proven.

I would not anger God any further with thy proof.

Aye, nor do I volunteer to find her!

*Elyas, she comes for her boy. Mayhap we give him her and she
leaves us be?*

Aye! Blacwin speaks sense! We send the lad into the wheat!

And when the Bailiff hears of it?

You fear Bailiffs more than ghosts? Jenny, hast you lost thine wits?

*Ah, Simon! Why did you anger Alice by noising those rumours of
her poisoning?*

*I did not! It was Clarice who turned her back upon Alice at the
Mill!*

*Lies! Do not forget it was to William that Henry Payne first
begged to share those additional lands, and Bill cried off!*

*What else could I do? I already had o'er much land. Jurors, this
mess be yours. Ye burdened that family so!*

Agreed! Denis, you abuse thy station!

*Oh, did I? Prithee, Osgoode, did you also hold this opinion when
you came grovelling to my door and begged reduction in thine own
obligations?*

Slander!...

76

       ...Friends, mayhap ye recall the moment earlier in my tale, when Pearl and I fled the Legumen-Woodwose in the forests of the Venison Lord. Pearl's words —*We tell tales of what lurks out in the dark so that we need not acknowledge the truth lurking within.*

Pearl had not believed me when I said I understood his meaning. But I did, friends. Truly I did, for I was remembering those nights in the Deepslough loft, listening to the village bickering. They feared Alice Payne out in the darkness, while never admitting their own roles in her exile. It was the same in Herthepoll, the honest poor of Sturdy Row turning against the Sturdy Beggars whose likewise poverty they believed deepened their own. It was the same as Ralf's evil grin and Joan taunting me with that salt pork pottage. It was the same as all those who look't upon me not as an orphan, but the offspring of an undead ghost.

Aye, when Pearl said it, I knew it to be true...

                        ...The Fiend

be our fault...

77

       ...A fiend I had still not seen for myself. But did I wish to? Though I miss't Mam more each day, could I witness her brok-armed and gory as they described?

Then it occurred there might be another way to bring her

close to me—her ale. At the completion of a brew, Mam would drynke from a cup afore passing it to me to do likewise. Our communal sup meant drynking down into ourselves a part of the other, for we had made the ale together. Thus, thought I, if I imbibed her ale, I could make her real once more...

78

...After another night of worried drynking, when all had left the Deepslough hame, I enacted my plan. Mask't by the snorings of Ralf, Joan, and their boys in the opposite loft, I creak't down the ladder from my own. Creeping to the ale barrel—much depleted by Joan's patrons—I spooned a quantity into a cup then slip't out into the warm summer night.

I skirted the cow enclosure and sat upon a tree stump. Though I had not gone far, the Cooper's iron hoop—tight about my chest for so long now—loosened somewhat. I look't up to the sparkling firmament, the moon casting pewter light across the village and open fields beyond. Then, ale cup in both hands, I drank deep of my mother.

Though it tasted some degree different—a faint tang in the throat—it was familiar enough that I could shut mine eyes and fly back to her. Back to Da and Christopher. Back to Robert and Sibyl, too, for they were also my blood...

...Friends, grief be a seed sown deep. Years might pass afore its sorrowful tendrils entwine themselves about thy heart. But entwine they shall, for it be a hardy plant that takes root in all climes. Drynking the ale that night, I felt truly knowledge long understood, but not reckoned with—I had lost my family.

I had lost them.

I wept and drank, drank and wept. What would become of me? Years more at the whims of the Deepsloughs, aye, that was certain...but after I came of age and inherited Da's lands and obligations, what then? Would I work them as he had? As the Paynes of Segerston had always done? Most likely, aye. But still, what *then?*

Was that all there was...?

...The ale was stronge, and I had sup't the cup dry. The village dizzied and became strange. I rose from the stump to return to the Deepsloughs, which was when I saw it...

...saw *her*...

...In the wheat...

...Twisted arms dangling...

...She tilted her head up to the moon, as if that globe spoke honeyed words I could not hear. Words which compelled me draw closer, to the edge of the wheat. There we look't at each other—for how long I cannot say—both of us weaving on the spotte. Her mooned eyes glittered in the dark collapse of her face. From deep in my chest, pressure built. Not a scream, but song—

You be loved

178

Hear my plea...

...The melody flowed
unforce't—

You be loved
You be me...

...flowed with a
sweetness I thought I would never again find—

'Til we meet
Once again...

...and when it reach't
the one in the wheat—

In my love...

...she began—

Never end...

...turning in slow,
syrupful circles, the wheat hushing about her. When my song
ended, she held out her arms. One was twisted so the hand
bend back at terrible angle. The other dangled by strings at the
elbow, jutting bone agleam through bloodless flesh. Towards
her shattered embrace I was pulled as the world span faster,
faster still. And I was almost there when, like a dagger plunged
deep, my stomach cramp't. I drop't to mine knees in the wheat

and spewed what felt like gallons, far more than I had imbibed. When it was all out and I regained mine feet, she was gone. Only a black patch of crop to say she had ever been there at all...

79

...The next moment, I awoke back in the loft, bone-tired, head walloping as Ralf demanded I move my idle arse. Descending the rickety ladders, I thought, had that been a dream? I recalled the words of the one-eyed Gleeman. Last night, had mine eyes seen that?

Or my heart?

I had not tyme to untangle it, for Osbert was at the door. He had never fetch't me during daylight, and when I arrived at the manor, I was fain surprised, Sacrist, to see thy carriage there, and several Monks sat patiently inside...

80

...Sacrist, how many long years lie 'twixt that day and this? Much hath occurred in the world since. England be again at war with France. The Scots raze Northumbria. Heretical Lollards threaten our souls, while rising prices do likewise our flesh. Though as I speak, Sacrist, mayhap things be not so different after all. Mayhap Fate's wheel hath turned one complete gyration, and the only change be the creases upon our faces? The snow in our hair?

Well, so be it.

Do you recall that day in the manor house? I do, for what

rustic could forget meeting the Sacrist of Durham? His very own Lord! The shuttered windows were opened, ushering in air and sunbeams for mayhap the first tyme since Thomas had been installed, and the light made thy white cassock shine in that dim, musty place. Dust billowed when you sat in Thomas' chair, while the Bailiff himself lurk't in the corner, looking more toadlike than ever. Thy arrival seemed not to have been telt to him aforehand because the dining table still heap't high with mess. But you were not looking at that, Sacrist. You were looking at me.

Childe, you said. *I need thy help in a grave matter. But first, are you God's servant?*

I attend Matins and Mass and Evensong, I replied.

Most do, but though their bodies stand in church, their minds— their hearts—be elsewhere.

I thought of Father Bell on his knees 'neath the painted chancel arch, and the Gleeman's milky eye upon me. Sacrist, I then made myself meet *thy* eye.

I have uprooted the tares from my wheat and disposed of them.

Sacrist, how you jounce't at my proclamation!

That gladdens me, you said. *For it ensures truthful answers to mine questions, the first being when did you last see thy mother?*

I did not expect this. Sacrist, you place't thy soft hand upon my shoulder.

When, lad? When did you last see her?

In an ale barrel, said I. *Sinking.*

You sighed. *Drynke ruins many a rustic.*

Then thy hand moved up my neck, cupping the back of my head.

But hast you witness't a figure abroad at night?

Aye.

Which you believe is thy mother?

I...Sacrist, I...

Boy, growled Thomas from the corner. *Mind who—*

Sacrist, one look stowed the Bailiff's wine-black tongue.

Look upon me, childe, not him. Is she thy mother Alice Payne?

I wept like a childe, for I was a childe. Sacrist, you allowed this without stirring to anger. You went to the open window, spoke to the Monks in the carriage. When I had finish't sobbing, you turned to me.

I ask, you said, *for I wish save her.*

Osbert ushered in a Monk carrying a parcel wrap't in a white shroud. Though it was only the size of a loaf, the Monk struggled with his load, dropping it onto the table with an almighty thump. Sacrist, you ask't me to remove the shroud. The fabric was near-pellucid 'neath mine besmirching fingers as I revealed the object—a quantity of metal pounded into a sheet and folded o'er, much as the shroud had been folded o'er it in turn.

Sacrist, you saw my confusion.

A Scroll of Absolution, you said. *Written by the Bishop of Durham himself. It is wrap't in a parcel of protective lead, to be place't on thy mother's chest as we bury her. Doing this shall absolve her of the sin now driving her rotted corpse across the land. For death without shrift or housel, son, it need not mean eternal expulsion from Heaven.*

At this, the Bailiff prick't his ears and listened as you continued.

Ye rustics forget this truth. And when tested, ye all turn not to God but to the dim days of your paganism. To false gods and superstition. That is why thine neighbours wish butcher thy mammy—to

*hack away her head. If that happens, she is lost for all tyme. Do you
wish that?*

I do not.

*Me neither, son. Thy mother is no monster, but a lost soul in need
of Absolution. And when this Scroll grants her safe passage to Purgatory, Segerston shall see that only through Christ does salvation
lie. And they shall chafe against God's design no more.*

You sat back in thy chair.

*But to do this, lad, we must know her location. Did she speak of
her lair?*

She did not speak, Sacrist.

I saw frustration upon thy face, Sacrist. Thought rapidly
mastered.

*Understandable, for walking ghosts are rarely loquacious. Other
channels of communication are better suited. Thomas tells me you
dream?*

I could only nod.

*Dreams loosen the tongues of the dead. Mayhap she hast spoken
to thee in dream?*

Thy irritation returned when I said nay. Though I pray you
believed me then, as I hope you believe me now. The thought of
Mam mouldering in the gorse, desperate for Absolution...that
wound never heals. But as a boy, looking upon that lead-wrap't
Scroll, I was ashamed. You wish't me to help save her, and I had
no answers to give. Still, Sacrist, in thy kindness, you did not
drive me to greater lamentation.

*I have also been told you sing, you said. Would you, afore I return
to the city?*

Distraught as I was, it was in my power to grant this
request. So I sang the song Mam had sung to me—the one I had

sung to Thomas, and to the one in the wheat. When I finish't, you press't a coin into my palm. Then you address't the Bailiff.

The Scroll remains here until we find her. I shall arrange men to search the fells.

I can arrange it, Sacrist.

Sacrist, the look you gave Thomas made the man melt like bubbling lard.

No, Bailiff, I do not believe thee can. You shall hear from my Cellarer anon...

81

...Sacrist, you left in the carriage and when Osbert shoved me outside, I ran to the Bishop's wall where you and I, Walter, had once spent many gay hours. There, I opened my fist to see the groat. Four pence—more money than I had ever held. I buried it 'neath a horn-shaped rock, and returned to the Deepsloughs...

82

...But the moment I was free of Ralf's labours the next day—and every day after—I was out upon the fells, Sacrist, searching with thine men. We look't in each ditch and crevice, 'neath every heather and rock, and though the vast fells met the horizon, I refused to extinguish my hope for one simple reason. The Scroll of Absolution. You, Sacrist, had brought it to Segerston *in person*—a man of thy stature and Godliness—thus its power was assured. God *himself* was in

that Scroll, and only God could bend my step in Mam's direction. I tried to clear my mind of grief and pain, so that I might
feel his guiding hand upon my back. Visions consumed me.
Visions of finding her lying abroad the fells in torment, of
placing the Scroll upon her chest and reading the Absolving
prayer so that her soul, now saved, burst from its cage of rotted
flesh and flew to Purgatory, where her hysband and sons and
daughter awaited.

Where they would all one day be waiting for me.

Yet thine men search't for weeks and found her not. The
nights grew long, and they returned to Durham for goode.
Sacrist, I do not blame thee. In dede, I wish now to thank thee,
for I did not get the chance then. Though thine men never found
Mam for to grant her salvation, Sacrist, you were *my* salvation.
If not for that single coin you gave to me, the man afore thee
now—the Gleeman named Mother Naked—would not exist...

...Mother Naked...

                        ...This name of mine, it hath mark't my
long lyf. In dede, many of ye Mercers laugh't when ye heard it,
so mayhap now be the tyme to reveal its origin. But friends—
after all I have said this night, can ye still not guess?

Nay? That saddens me.

So allow me to grieve further...

83

                        ...As Lancaster
Lambert experimented with his apothecary syrups, so Pearl

and I spent the early days of our association in composition of our act. He was the greater psaltery player, while I possess't a sweeter voice. Yet even once these elements had been mix't, the elixir was far from finish't. I was young—barely twelve— and lacking Gleeman experience, aye, but in other ways also was I fain raw. Segerston still harrowed my mind. Nightly, I drownded in my mother's ale barrel, gasping awake, clawing at my breast. I was afeard of the world, and of my own name. In each town, my partner would grandly introduce himself to the crowd—*Greetings, friends, I be Pearl Eye the Gleeman!*—but I knew not what to say. Segerston was ruined, and I was a villein on the run. As in Herthepoll, had my name been noised to the local Sheriffs? Were the hounds already upon my trail?

So I gave no name to any audience.

Anon, Pearl grew vex't at this anonymous, snivelling wretch who had attach't himself to his person. One evening, while supping away the day's purse in some tavern, he gave me a choice—take a name and live up to it, or leave him. I did not wish the latter, for gruff as he was, Pearl was all I had. Yet none of the names I slip't like tunics o'er myself seemed to fit. I no longer knew who I was, so how should I know what garment to wear? Seeing my distress, Pearl softened. For the first and only tyme, he telt me how he had found the name Pearl Eye. Friends, ye remember the story I telt—of his father Gervase, the high-rank't Gleeman, and their fall into destitution when a more famous player arrived at the castle to usurp him.

Fordwin Blanchflower was his name, said Pearl. *Yet when he first came, my father was not troubled. After all, he had served Roger de Colton long and well, as generations of our family had done. So why fear? He even extended friendship to Fordwin, and bade me do likewise to his son, a childe named Melchior. But Melchior* did not like me, and I shall never forget his words—"You and thy father belong in some low tavern, banging pisspots. And when ye are expelled from this castle, no one shall remember your crude clan."

Said I to Pearl, *Melchior was wrong to say such.*

Was he, now? Pearl replied. *For that prancing turd's prophecy came true. When Da returned from the tavern to whatever hovel we were then living in, and began beating me, sometymes he muttered aloud the fragments of his thoughts. Some plot, he was sure, had been enacted against him at Appleby Castle. Some ploy cook't up by Fordwin to turn Roger de Colton against him. As a lad, I believed him. But now...now I reckon Da knew different, and drynke was his only escape from the truth.*

What truth? said I. Remember, friends, I was young then.

That Roger chose Fordwin Blanchflower o'er him for no other reason than it took his fancy. That to the rich, our names mean naught and shall be forgotten regardless.

When he saw I did not comprehend, he closed his goode eye. Staring at me with his milky dead one—the eye his father had blinded in drunken rage—Pearl spoke.

So take a name YOU cannot forget...

...That night, I dreamed of my mother again. Of her shedding her rags and lowering her battered flesh into the barrel. At the fayre the next day, Pearl introduce't himself to the crowd, and when it was my turn, where I had previously hidden away, I now step't forth and in full throat sang my name. The only one that fit...

...*Mother Naked, at your service*...

84

...The cinders of September 1397 had cooled to October ashes, and a chill fog roiled pottage-thick about Joan's tavern that final night of its existence. In my loft, I look't down upon a brooding room of rustics with hollow cheeks and huge, black pupils; their eerie pall brok only by occasional whimpers and crack't giggling. But was this trancement caused by the Wraith? Or a simpler terror? For in church that day, wine-bloated Thomas had read out the manor's demesne Reap Roll for the year—grim yields lower than Segerston had seen in a century. Likewise, the villagers' own lands had produce't barely enough to carry most beyond Christmastide. *The harvest fails*, said the Bailiff as he staggered away, *and ye fukkit rustics, now ye starve.*

In the tavern that was his hame, his tenure as Reeve ended in calamity, Ralf sprawled upon the floor. He had been guzzling ale all day, as had Joan, sat upon her stool by the fyre with cup in hand, trance't by the flames. She had abandoned her role as Taverness, so her patrons had to lurch to the barrel and scoop their own cup. But not for much longer, for I had brewed all my father's grain, and her own supplies were about gone. Joan was down to her final barrel, and the chances of making more were as remote as her mind, for she seemed as stupefied as all the rest.

In dede, the only man to rouse himself was the freeman George Goodsell, he whose son would hath likely gone to Duncan Harpour until Adelbert Attwell played his hand. All night, George's gob had been chewing upon itself. He was building up to speak his mind, which, in his drunken befuddlement, must hath felt like herding poultry. Finally, though, he had his words marshalled, and spoke in terms queerly similar to what I would one day hear beside the forest of a Woodwose.

Adelbert, said George. *False-man thou...This fiend be thy fault.*

This inspired a second freeman—his name I remember not—to wake from his trance and continue the sluggish onslaught.

Attwell...by God's nails, you hast brought this...horror upon...us.

From his position face down 'neath the table, groaned a third freeman.

Adelbert Attwell...

...frigger...

...of...

...gooooooooatttsssssss...

...Walter, scarcely does it need be said that such vile defamations were birth't by logic untethered from reason. In their ale-addled minds, the freemen blamed thy father for informing the Bailiff of Alice Payne's whereabouts in Herthepoll, an event leading to her grisly, unshriven death, and subsequent resurrection as a vengeful ghost.

Though they continued slinging accusation at poor Adelbert, I was unsure how much the man comprehended. For since the Wraith's return, this once-abstinent man had drunk more ale than any other. Was it his guilt o'er Alice Payne? *Did* he blame himself, as others blamed him? Or was it the thought of the ruined future ahead? Walter, be thankful you were not there to see thy father in such state, nor thy mother either. For Mabel had also succumbed to the Wraith's corrupting influence, and spent her days in depressive mood upon her pallet. She was not in the tavern that night when, from my loft, I observed the middle Deepslough brother, Theobald, rise from his table, clutching his guts. The door was o'er far away, so he push't open a window shutter to blow a bellyful into the foggy night. He stayed that way—his top half hanging out into the vaporous air—for some tyme, afore pulling his head back inside...

...Now, it be my experience with drynke that, while spewing itself be a grim act, the sensation after purging be quite agreeable. Yet Theobald seemed worse, not better. Hand trembling, he pick't up a cup and shuffled to the half-empty ale barrel. He leaned inside to fill it, speaking as he did, so the barrel's cavity redoubled the sound of his voice.

She's come, then.

Theobald's barrel-voice bludgeoned through the thickened wits of some, including George Goodsell. The freeman heaved himself to his feet and tottered unsteadily to the wall, which was pegged with the many tools required of villeinage. He brought down a scythe. Those still awake watch't George put the deadly article upon the table afore Adelbert.

You started her, said George. *You end her.*

But Adelbert still did not fully grasp the situation. That moment only arrived, Walter, when George closed thy father's fists around the shaft of the scythe, dragged him to his feet, and thrust him to the door.

Nay, whimpered Adelbert. *I cannot.*

Then I shall take that scythe...and lop off thine culls.

Walter, thy da had never struck a violent blow to aught but stubborn oxen. But now he went into the foggy night to destroy the Wraith.

After he left, the tavern fix't their wide, blown-out eyes upon the door. Nobody breathed. And just as I thought Adelbert had done a flit, there came from outside a terrible shriek. Some drynkers moaned in fear, others wept. Slump't upon his table, Stephen the Miller began pissing his hose as the door creak't open...

...But it was only Adelbert returned. Dark blood soak't his tunic, his hands, his face. The blade of his scythe drip't freely with it.

Something in...the fog, whispered Adelbert. *So I...slice't out...*
She be dead? ask't George.
She fled...towards the manor. But it was not...she was not...
Speak, Adelbert? What was she not?

Adelbert shambled back to his table and lowered the gory scythe upon it, as if setting down a feast-day suckling.

Adelbert! cried George. *What was she not?!*

Sitting down, Adelbert folded his head into his arms and began to laugh...

...And laugh...

...And laugh...

...And did not stop even as Ralf Deepslough rose from the floor, all manner of straws and shite stuck to him, and pick't up the scythe Adelbert had only just put down.

By the bloody shtate of thish blade, slurred Ralf, *I should shay*

the cunte Alice Payne hath jigged her last. Which means...it be tyme
her little lad joinsh her...

Ralf stood at the bottom of the ladder to my loft, waving the
scythe up at me.

Come down and join ush, lambkin?

I shrank back upon the creaking boards.

Timid cur, said Ralf. *Then I shall come up to thee...*

The ladder shook as he climbed. Terrified, I search't
the thatch for an exit—some rent or hole I might squeeze
through—but it was pack't snug. Then the scythe's murdering
blade appeared, followed by its long shaft and the malicious
slab of Ralf's head.

His thick shoulders and trunk.

His legs.

Feet.

There was not room for him to stand in the loft, so he
crouch't as if peering into a rabbit's warren at the mewling
creature cowering within. Black pupils like two wells bored
into his face, his thick lips gurning as he crawled to me.

Bairn, I put thee to goode use. Now our pigs be dead, I shall salt
thee down for meat.

Ralf jabbed the blade at me.

I shall make it quic—

The loose and rotted boards that barely supported my feeble
weight gave way 'neath Ralf's bulk. He tumbled from my sight,
hitting the pack't earth with the deep crack a boar jointed by
a Butcher. Though I wish't not to, I peered o'er the planks and
saw Ralf upon the ground, his neck twisted abominably.

Bertram, the youngest brother, got to his feet. The Wraith's
sickness was heavy upon him, but he did not go to his father's
corpse. Nay, Bertram's gob slackened at the sight of his mam,

for though Joan Deepslough remained seated by the fyre in the middle of the room, the left side of her face was gone—slice't off by the scythe tumbling from Ralf's hand as he fell—and in its place, a glistening horror of meat, muscle, bone.

And I swear to every Mercer in this room, I *swear* Joan continued sitting upon that stool, hands prim about her ale cup, and her eye—the remaining eye in her face—went on staring into the fyre, and *blink't* once...

...twice...

...thrice...

...Afore she fell forward into the blaze...

...Friends, greasy auld Joan in her greasy auld clothes went up quick. The room billowed with unctuous smoke, a sight—and smell—which trance't the room in its evil spectacle. But not Bertram.

Maaaaam! came his lamentable cry.

Which was when he made his fatal error.

He lurch't o'er to his mother, now full ablaze. Ignorant of the heat, Bertram grip't her waist, intending, I believe, to haul her from the inferno. But he misjudged her weight and o'er-balanced himself, falling forwards into the fyre to wallop his skull against the hearth-stones. His wits snuff'd out, he roasted with his mother...

...I descended the loft in thickening smoke, thanking God that when Ralf had fallen, the ladder did not. I ran for the door 'twixt dazed drynkers, some of who were attempting to stand as if in waking sleep. Most, though, seemed incapable of movement—their moony eyes following me as I reach't the door. When I did, there came a terrible groaning from the opposite loft.

Philip Deepslough look't down.

He floundered limply upon his front, one arm dangling o'er the edge. Slaver hung from his gob as, with huge black eyes, he surveyed the ruination of his family. Joan and Bertram crisping in the fyre. Ralf with his head twisted backwards. And in the corner, Theobald's legs sticking out of the ale-barrel, where, after announcing the Wraith's arrival, he had fallen in head-first and drownded.

Philip saw it all.

Then he saw me.

Yooooooouuuu, he moaned.

Surveying the carnage, George Goodsell spoke as if he no longer knew where he was.

Adelbert said...the fiend fled...to the manor...

I fled too. And the last sound I heard was not Philip's anguish't howl, but thy father, Walter. Adelbert Attwood...

...Laughing, laughing, laughing...

85

...Lo! My gruesome tale upsets yonder Mercer, for he staggers from the hall like he hath been supping Joan's ale! Mayhap my bloody tale hath upset the man's urbane refinement? After all, ye Mercers—Sacrist, Walter, Hugh, too—ye inhabit a world inverse to the one I describe.

Your dainty silks and gilded linens, they let you drape this lyf in what it be not. Well, friends, allow me to strip away the fabrics so that ye elegant cuntes might behold the shite below...

...What, nobody grutches at my insolence? That be a first, for ye have moaned like spoilt bairns all night—*Mother, how dare you speak to us thusly? Mother, do not say that! Mother, who do you think thee be?* Well, *friends,* I think I be the only man in this hall without slaver upon his chin, for ye all now look fain sick. *Goode.* Feel sicker as I finish my tale. I would say we ought wait for your friend who just now left, but I fancy that be the last ye ever see of him. Besides, the hour be late and we have arrived at the sharp end of things. So let us plunge it deep...

86

...I fled the Deepslough hame into fog so thick I could see naught as I ran, then trip't o'er something upon the ground—a bloody, outstretch't arm. Mine eyes followed the arm to the shoulder, where lay connected the rest of Mabel Attwell. A ragged gash from gut to gullet slit up her front. White face frozen in perpetual scream. Likely, my own scream would not hath been so silent, but as I was about to let it fly, a rough hand smothered my gob.

Master wants thee, said Osbert.

I twisted and kick't but that did not trouble the Valet. He threw me upon his shoulder and cut swift through the mist to the manor, as if guided not by eyes, but sneck. For in truth that was what Osbert was. A bloodhound, gelded...

87

...Walter,
I cry pardon about thy mother, for there be no crueller dea—
Lo! a Mercer crashes to the floor! Why, it be the fellow with
the drooping whiskers whom I spoke with earlier, he who
hath waged a dozen Priests in his will. Droopy, look at thee—
sprawled upon the flags like a fukkit *dog*. Get up, man. Hast
you no *pryde?* Nay, of course you do not, so I shall drag thee
back into thy seat...

...Umf...

...Well, well, well, Droopy.
Mayhap you hadst a weak heart, for it seems those Priests
shall be singing thy name sooner than imagined. Though in
vain. And this be what I was saying to thee, Walter—there
be no crueller death than a sudden one. Now you know what
happened to my own mother, you see I understand that better
than most. I promise't to end those low rumours that it was
thy father who killed thy mother, and I believe I have done so,
for they be rumours no more. Adelbert swung the scythe in
belief he was ending the Wraith, not his wyf. A tragedy, Walter,
though at least thee now know it. The rents in the fabric of
thy understanding be sewn shut.

More than most of us get, that.

And take heart, Walter. Though Mabel died without shrift
and housel, hope remains. The Sacrist once procured a Scroll
of Absolution for my mother, so mayhap he shall do so for thy
own. Why not ask him...?

...Walter...?

...*Walter*, you
bastard, do you hear me...?

...There be a flicker in thine
eyes, so I know thee can. Friends, it seems many of ye have
fallen likewise into reverie, and remain fix't in your chairs.
Allow me, then, to reward your attentiveness...

88

...The manor
house hove out of the fog. Osbert carried me through the back
door and lock't it behind us, then toss't me alone into the room
where I usually entertained his Master, locking it likewise. I
expected to find the typical mess—a drunken Thomas idling
by the fyre—but nay. Though it was lit by only a fewe candles
in their stone alcoves, I saw the room had been emptied of
its usual wreckage. The stone floors were scoured, the table
cleared of mouldering bowls and bottles, papers and parch-
ments. But the table was not empty, for Thomas himself lay
spreadeagle upon it with limbs lash't to its four legs. Upon his
chest, bound likewise with ropes, was the lead parcel contain-
ing the Scroll of Absolution.

Thomas could not turn his head, so spoke to the ceiling.
Closer, lad.

I approach't the table. By his side, two objects—a paper
and a dagger. With wheeling horror, I knew then what this
was about.

Thomas, I said. *I cannot.*

The Cellarer was right, said he. *God delivered me from death so that I might do goode. But look about this village. What goode have I done?*

You tried, said I.

Not enough. Thus, the remaining half of my soul falls to Hell. Fragmented souls are forbidden entrance to Heaven so, come Final Judgment, God shall send the half now languishing in Purgatory to meet its brother in the Pit.

Thomas quivered and sweated as he spoke. For the first tyme since I had met the man, he had taken no drynke.

The Sacrist brought this Scroll for Mam, said I.

He brought it for a soul in torment.

His breath was thin 'neath the crushing weight upon his chest. The ropes groaned as he strained against them. The Valet had tied the knots well.

Thomas, can Osbert not fulfil this request?

Nay, said Thomas. *Such a coarse man cannot be party to this. Besides, he is not lettered and stumbles o'er a simple Paternoster. Nobody else in this village can read. It must be you, lad. I know the magnitude of what I ask, for I...I have wronged thee greatly. I cry pardon for that. Truly. But I beg thee, take up the knife.*

The blade glimmered in the candledark as I did so.

When I am dead, said Thomas, *read aloud the Prayer of Absolution as it is written upon the paper.*

Hand shaking, I put the knife to his neck. A tear slid from Thomas' eye.

There is no shame in being afeard, he said. *I am afeared.*

I felt the whet edge against his flesh. The slightest movement, and he would be gone.

Thomas, prithee, I...

198

I always wanted a son, he said. *A boy who could face down this bitter world as I never could. And thee, I believe you can.*

But I could not. I let go the knife and buried my face into his neck. There, I wept for my family and the cruelty we had endured. And I wept o'er their deaths—the rage and sadness and guilt of it—for though Thomas said he was to blame, I blamed myself more.

I know not how long I press't my face to the Bailiff's flesh, but when I was spent, Thomas was weeping too.

Forgive me, he said. *Oh, forgive me. It is cruel to put this on thee, and how I have made a lyf of such cruelty. But I can see no other path to salvation.*

At that, I lifted my head and look't into his glistening eyes.

Mayhap there be one.

Perplexity upon his countenance.

How?

Not how, Thomas. Who—me. Shew God you hast not spurned his second chance by taking care of me. Make amends, achieve redemption.

Fresh tears spilled down his temples.

As might a...father?

I nodded.

Then cut mine ropes.

I did so with the knife. Grunting, Thomas heaved the lead-wrap't Scroll from his chest and got down from the table. I let him pull me into a shaking embrace, then he took an iron key from his person and unlock't the door.

Osbert shall make thee a bed upstairs.

First, I ought tell the Deepsloughs that I stay with you now.

Aye, he said. *Aye, do that.*

He unlock't the back door and let me out. Upon his face was

a smile, tremulous but hopeful. It was the first—and last—tyme I would see him such.

I shall see thee anon, said he...

...In thick fog, I ran around the side of the manor, following the curve of the heugh 'til it climbed south towards Durham. The wall of the Bishop's deer park appeared to my left and, eventually, I came to my clearing. Sacrist, thy groat lay where I had hidden it 'neath the horn-shaped rock. I held it, glinting, in my filthy palm. But I had no tyme to wash it. Instead, I did what you, Walter, hadst always dared me do—I pulled myself onto the wall and prepared to flee into those forbidden lands. But afore I did, I took a last look back at Segerston. Through trees and fog, I was stunned to see the manor ablaze. That was all I saw. No movement. No sound—just silent, burning fog. I thought of the field in Matthew's Parable. I had uprooted mine tares, but had not incinerated them. Instead, I had done something else with those weeds, so did the manor now burn in their place? Or had Thomas done this? I thought not, for never had I seen the man as happy as when I left him. So if not the Bailiff, who?

It was then I saw the silhouette against the flames. A figure turning towards me.

So I drop't down the other side of the wall and was gone...

89

...Fie, a Mercer o'er there laughs as if I speak *comedy*. And he be not alone. Others titter queerly like the rustics of Segerston during those final months. But that cannot be, can it? For the

Wraith be not here. I must infer, then, ye be in possession of odd humour, sirs, of which I shall not judge.

So I tax ye no further with mine exploits that night, and say only that, in the weeks following, I lived feral upon the roads. I filch't what I had to filch. Slept in barns, abandoned cottages, outhouses. The cold near crack't me. And though it might hath purchase't a fewe hot meals, a night at an inn with a warming fyre, I did not spend that groat. Sacrist, it became for me a charm. An anchor to lyf.

After all, a rustic be never more than a groat from the grave...

90

...I was finally parted from it in Alnwick when, as I was lurking in the shadows of the town square, alert to whatever scraps might be stolen as market pack't away, mine ears caught a hubbub from one corner—a man pounding upon the door of an inn, demanding entrance. I slip't around the square's edge and into the vennel separating the inn from its neighbour, so as to get a better view. The man appeared much dishevelled, with dried blood in his whiskers, his torn tunic thick with muck. As he slammed himself against the door, I saw I had met him not once, but twice—first at Segerston during the feast of Saint John, and again at Durham market. The tare-eating Gleeman. The one-eyed psaltery strummer. Though in Alnwick, he seemed to be without his instrument for reasons I learn't when the Inn-Keeper's head appeared from the upper window.

Gleeman, she said, *do you bring me what you owe?*
Helen, that be what I wish speak on. I had it, but then—
Then a fairie flew out thy arse and said, "Oh, me fairie-mam be

rotten sick and needs her fairie tonic. Will you buy it her?" Gleeman, you think I believe a fabulator of tales such as thee?

Tales? Look at me, Helen! I have been robbed and beaten by thieves.

By those you owe debts, more like. Not a dice-rattler for miles you hast not cross't.

Pearl flew at the door again. Helen laugh't.

Settle thy bill afore stepping foot in here, sweeting.

To do that, I need my means of earning.

That psaltery stays with me. And if I do not get what I be owed by the morrow, I shall hock it. Though what that wreck't thing fetches, I know not.

Panting hard, Pearl lowered himself to his knees in the muck and shite.

Find clemency in thy heart, Helen.

Find coins in thy purse, she replied and shut the window.

Pearl remained on bended knee, head low. He growled like a dog in dream, but when I made some squeak from the vennel, he leapt to his feet and demanded I come out afore he battered me. Much afeard, I did so. Pearl cock't his head in befuddlement.

You be familiar? said he.

Taking a breath, I sang, Wheat, tares, and Fat John—fine feast for the crows!

Pearl bark't laughter, hard and true.

I never forgot thine pipes! What be you fingering in this fine arsehole of Alnwick?

Not knowing quite why, I removed the Sacrist's groat from my tunic.

Pay the Inn-Keeper.

He rubbed his bruised jaw. Thank thee, but a groat won't sate that bitch. Keep it for...

His words fell away. Rubbing his jaw harder, he entered into stern conversation with himself until one side won out and he knelt beside me. The beating he had taken had been heavy, his blind eye nested in its swollen orbit. He stank of ale, of violence.

What be thy name, lad?

I telt it to him.

Pearl Eye be mine, said Pearl Eye. *Now we be finally fair met, mayhap I borrow that groat after all?*

He pluck't it from my palm and cut across the market. I struggled to keep pace as he wended his way through vennel and alley, stopping at a sagging building down a noxious backstreet. Rabble came from inside. Pearl bade me wait outside as he push't open the door, and I glimpse't jostling bodies around tables lit by low, greasy tallow. The skitter of dice and coarse oaths. Then the door shut and I was alone with the dogs rooting slops. Shivering, I slid down the wall, drew up mine knees. Mayhap I dozed, or mayhap Pearl did not tarry, for he was suddenly afore me again.

Come away lad, he said.

What happened?

Come away.

Back at the inn, he hoof't the door 'til the Inn-Keeper's head emerged again. Pearl rattled a purse and toss't it up. Silence as the woman counted and recounted the coins.

We be equal, Helen? ask't Pearl.

Helen vanish't. A minute later, she threw down Pearl's possessions into his arms, psaltery and all, afore slamming the window shut.

Pearl check't his instrument. Though there did not seem to be additional damage upon it, he look't troubled.

I was one cup of dice away from oblivion, he said. *How long can a man live so?*

His battered face was gaunt in the gloom as he saw my condition—my tattered tunic and starved cheeks. A sad smile touch't Pearl's lips, splitting them anew. Blood ran down his chin as he place't his hand upon my crown.

But forgive me, he said. *For I believe you already know the answer to that...*

91

...Pearl and I became a pair then, and stayed that way through many long, strange decades. From Bentham to Berwick-upon-Tweed we roamed, and all betwixt. In dede, the only place we never returned was Segerston. This was at my request, though that did not mean I was free of the place. I was not. O'er the years, Segerston came to find me—the legend of the Fell Wraith noised about every corner of Durham; its taverns, markets, common greens, even churches all a-blether with tales of that woman-thing swaying her wormy hips 'neath the moon.

Tales of my mother, I suppose.

And so I grew auld while she aged not one day more. Until I stand here now, friends, with white in my hair and grit in mine joints. Back aching. Head paining. Feet swollen.

At the end of an endless pilgrimage.

And I owe all to Pearl. For though we did bicker so, he shewed me this world's great wonder...

...Its great evil...

...I have seasoned my tale this night with a scattering of our adventures together, but it would take another lyftyme to tell of all Pearl and I saw together. But another lyftyme none of us here possess, so I shall leap to my friend's death and the conclusion of our story...

92

...Mercers, I cry pardon, but I miss't the Mystery Play which you performed earlier today, as you do each feast of Saint Godric. Though on my way to the cathedral, I spoke to some wight in the street who telt me ye chose for this year's performance Noah and the Great Flood. How apt for such a storm now raging outside!

Friends, Pearl's death involves your play of six years ago. Does any man here remember the subject of your performance...?

...Friends...?

...It seems ye have all succumbed to the same queer malady that befell Melchior Blanchflower. Plenty of glassy eyes and slack gobs! And at yonder head table—Hugh de Tanfield slumps sidewise onto gurgling Walter! Only you, Sacrist, remain lucid...but barely. Mayhap it be the drynke? Sacrist, how much did you sup? It be a fine drop, aye? Rich and sweet, yet with a *tang* at the back of the throat? I know you cannot answer me, Sacrist, but thee can still hear me—ye *all* can still hear me. So fret not, friends, for we—*ye*—be almost finish't...

93

...Friends, the play ye mounted six years gone was none other than the Death of Judas. Pearl and I were waged alongside a troupe of music men to perform melodies for the demise of that traitorous wight, and we were given stern direction by the play's chief architect— Walter Attwell, now lolling moon-eyed upon his chair. By then, Duncan Harpour was long dead and you, Walter, hadst taken o'er the procurement of the Sacrist's vestments. In this endeavour, you were even more renowned than your erstwhile Master. This was why you were so exacting upon the play's every detail, for it was how you likewise operated in matters of commerce.

From the start, you hated Pearl. You spoke harshly to him when he miss't his musical cues or struck discordant notes. Pearl did this often, though not for obstinate reasons like with the Hull Silversmiths. Rather, Pearl's faculties were now in decline. He was almost sixty, and a lyf of ceaseless travel had aged him yet further. Sixty be the age when a man ought seat himself afore a goode fyre. His *own* fyre. With family about to shoulder his burdens...but Pearl had no family. No fyre either, in hearth or heart. There was a rattle in his chest and even his goode eye was turning milky. At nights, wherever we were, he no longer slip't off to some boisterous tavern, but instead stayed close to me. The darkness frightened him, and as we lay down, he would whisper the contents of his mind.

Did we make a difference?
All that we saw.
Mother, was it worth it?

My only answer was to hold him 'til he slept, for his fate today would be mine the morrow...

...Only who will hold me...?

...Come the feast of Saint Godric, the city filled with revelry. The market square clamoured with Jongleurs, Tumblers, and Mummers as your Mercer-wagon rolled into position. I see many of that play's performers here this night. In dede, this fellow afore me here with piss down his leg, he did play Judas Iscariot!

Walter, you were not a player, but instead conducted the music which Pearl laboured to play. My friend's distress pained me, for music had once been to him as breathing...and now he struggled to do both. Stiff-fingered, he wrestled his psaltery, and in this fashion we reach't the play's summit, the scene all had come to witness.

Judas' demise.

Friends, ye shall recall that, as part of his dedication to perfection, Walter had used thirty pieces of real silver in the purse Judas earned for betraying Jesus with a kiss in the Garden of Gethsemane. And when, in repentance, Iscariot attempted to return the curse't bounty to the Temple Officers, Walter, in thy genius, you hadst sewn the purse with false-seams so it would split in stryking fashion, scattering coins when he hurled it at the feet of Christ's persecutors. This the purse duly did, but one of the silver coins rolled from the stage and fell to the ground.

Not many folk saw it happen, for all eyes were fix't upon Judas. But a gaunt vagabond girl—a childe from the waste-strewn vennels—she saw the coin come to rest by one wheel of the wagon. Like a flashing trout, she darted 'neath the vehicle and palmed it, only for *you*, Walter, to block her escape. As the music swelled and Judas put the noose about his neck, Walter grabbed the lass. When she bit thee, Walter, you slap't her hard across the face and rifled her rags for the coin. That you would hast found it anon there can be no doubt, but then Pearl appeared.

Walter, my first thought was Pearl intended to stryke thee, for in years gone I had seen him snuff many a man's wits. But now Pearl was auld and infirm, so instead of swinging his fist, he tried getting 'twixt thee and the lass, so that you could not harm her. This vex't thee, Walter, so you struck Pearl a blow to the temple. My friend stumbled back, but his disruption was enough—the girl twisted free of thy grip and vanish't into the crowd with her bounty.

But what of me, friends? Where was I during this business? I swear, I wanted to help Pearl—was bending my step in his direction—when I spotted someone in the bright May sunlight. A woman clothed in gory rags, lank hair hanging o'er her face, she swayed her hips, and her brok arms—false ones made from tied sticks—swung as the Fell Wraith Mummer dance't towards me.

And as she did, mine legs became jelly...

...This trance was only brok by a cry of pain behind the stage, and I saw *that man there*—auld Droopy Whiskers now dead in his chair—I saw *him* bending Pearl's arm, for aside from being a Mercer, he was also a Sheriff's Constable. Droopy smack't Pearl several tymes, tore the psaltery from his hands, and hauled him away in the direction of North Gate gaol...

94

...But I avoid the question
—*why* did I not save Pearl? Had the sight of the Fell Wraith
Mummer shaken me to inaction, or was she merely the closest
excuse to hand? The answer be a simple one—Pearl was born
with culls, and I was not. He *writhed* in lyf. Lived in the jagged,
screaming teeth of it, whereas I have always been a watcher by
inclination. An observer. Queer, given my Gleeman profession,
but mayhap that be the truth of cowardice—you spend thy
whole span making sense of it. Making peace with it. Making
apology for it. Thus, I have spent this night *speaking* to you rich
cuntes when, just as Pearl had struck Hull Jesus, a fist does
better.

But Pearl be dead.

Ye bastards killed him...

95

...Well, as Judas swung from
his bough, I scoop't up my friend's psaltery and followed Constable Droopy dragging Pearl away. Beyond the meaty stench
of Flesheweregate, they entered North Gate gaol. I slip't into
a vennel as I had done in Alnwick, only things were different
now. Pearl was different. I was different.

We were auld.

When it became dark and Pearl had yet to emerge, I found
mine shrivelled culls and entered the gaol to ask the Guard
about my friend. This fair and pleasant soul, who smelt worse

that the offal-merchants down the street, he wasted no tyme in instructing me to frig my mother's holes. I returned to my spying vennel 'til, late that evening, Droopy left the gaol alone, and I threw myself at his feet to beg for word. Sneering, he telt me Pearl had been amerce't three shillings and was being detained until he paid. I went immediately to the hock-shop and gave o'er my psaltery. Then, with Pearl's instrument in mine arms, I spent the next week playing every tavern in the city. I played and sang until I was fainting away, then, upon waking, I played again. I played 'til mine fingers blebbed and my voice brok. 'Til, finally, I returned to the gaol with the coin to free my friend...

...When I saw Pearl again, I knew his lyf was short. The rattle in his chest had congealed, and all about his body were sores and bruises. But that was not the worst of it. The bones of his right hand had been crush't—stamp't upon by booted feet—meaning Pearl would never play his psaltery again...

96

...A kind freeman took us in his cart as he journeyed past Lumley castle. Lancaster had by then died, making his second son, Marmaduke, the Lord, as he be to this day. Fortunately, Marmaduke shared his father's bent for medicinal arts and, in dede, had widened and refined Lancaster's repertoire of concoctions.

Marmaduke's servants made a bed for Pearl, while he set to work healing his injuries. He knew death would soon come to the Gleeman, but to ease his pain the Lord attempted to apply a poultice. Clinging to his wits, Pearl shook his head.

Nay, croak't my friend. *I wish see something.*

See something? ask't Marmaduke.

Aye, like thy father on occasion made me see things.

Are you sure?

Never more so.

Clod that I be, I thought Pearl spoke of lighting more candles. But Marmaduke took off to his apothecary shelves, returning with a tray on which stood two large leather bottles, and a third smaller one.

Wine or ale? ask't Marmaduke.

You be the Physikian.

From one of the large bottles, Marmaduke poured a cup of ale. Next, he held the small bottle o'er the cup 'til a dark syrup droop't from the aperture into the brew.

Lord Marmaduke, said I, *Lancaster made fine Devils-bit syrup. This does not look as that.*

Because it is not syrup of Devils-bit, but syrup of darnel.

Darnel? The weed?

One and the same.

Marmaduke stirred the ale and, tilting Pearl's head, help't him drynke. As he did, I remembered Pearl's words to me at market.

He shall see what his heart sees, I said.

Marmaduke look't at me queerly. *True, the plant hath strange properties. When ingested, it grants visions. Or mayhap not. Mayhap you see what is always there. Regardless, my reduction deepens the effects many tymes o'er.*

How much do you give him?

Two or three thimblefuls only. More, and you risk breaking a man's wits eternally.

A further question came to me.

What if the syrup be not mix't into ale, but WAS ale? Darnel malted like normal grain and fermented to ale in the usual fashion?

Marmaduke considered this.

The effect would not be as rapid, but if enough ale was consumed o'er tyme then, aye, it ought work the same.

I had used darnel for Joan's ale because she had scant grain to brew, and because Pearl once telt me it could be ingested. In truth, though, I had also brewed it for another reason— if darnel made the heart see what the eyes wish't not, well, I *wanted* Segerston to see. What that village did to my family— aye, I had wanted them to see that very well.

Noting my troubled expression, Marmaduke drew the wrong conclusion.

I would not suggest thee brew it, said he. *Disaster would likely await.*

Well, sir, I would not wish court that.

We sat by Pearl's bedside deep into the night. The man barely moved, barely drew breath. But by degrees, some animus returned. He sighed, though not unpleasantly. The darnel seemed to be taking effect; decades of weary travel melting from his bones. Pearl closed his eyes—one goode, one bad—and a smile formed upon his lips.

Lord Marmaduke, I said. *I thought darnel capable of granting only troubled visions?*

"He shall see what his heart sees," replied Marmaduke. *Mayhap his heart is glad?*

The Lord look't me up and down.

How is THY heart, Gleeman?

I do not know, said I.

Marmaduke daubed syrup onto his finger and suck't. He held out the bottle to me.

If you wish learn?

I declined his offer—as I say, first and foremost, I be an observer of lyf—but also because I wish't remain alert for my friend. During that night, the darnel took Pearl upon some wonderous journey 'neath the flit and flutter of his shuttered eyelids. Sometymes a laugh slip't from him, other tymes a tear cut the grime of his cheek. His unbroken hand would find mine and squeeze with ebbing strength...

...At Prime the next morn, Marmaduke fetch't for a Priest. The clergyman ask't Pearl's true name, and it struck me I did not know it. To me, he was—will always be—Pearl Eye. The Priest then attempted to shrive Pearl, and I fretted he might not wake. But the auld Gleeman opened his eyes.

I was curious to see what Pearl would do. Would the Lollard in him tell this Priest where he might shove his shrift and housel, those man-made barriers 'twixt man and God? But Pearl spoke calmly when the Priest ask't if his worldly affairs were ordered.

Mother, my psaltery belongs to thee.

It was then tyme for shrift.

Said the Priest, *What sins must you confess?*

My friend shut his eyes again. The Priest was about to repeat his question, when Pearl opened his blind eye. It moved o'er the Priest's shoulder to something invisible in the corner of the room.

Da, said Pearl. *How fare you?*

Nervous, the Priest look't to the empty corner, then to me, then back to Pearl.

I say again, said he, *what is thy confession?*

Pearl kept his dead eye on the corner.

Da, I cry pardon...I saw thee choking...and I let thee go...

From his pyx, the Priest removed the sacramental Host and place it upon Pearl's tongue. Pearl closed his gob. For a moment, I thought he was going to swallow, then he stuck out his tongue and took Christ's flesh from it, handing the soggy thing back to the Priest.

No thank thee...that was 'twixt Gervase and me...

Then Pearl laugh't.

Walter, it was not like thy father's moon-struck giggle. Nor Ralf's spiteful crow, nor Thomas the Bailiff's bitter snort.

It was the laugh of a man at ease...

...And he died anon, without shrift and housel...

...As a freeman finally free...

97

...Friends, who still be in their wits? Nobody? Now even the *Sacrist* seems rooted to his chair, slavering as if floored by some vision. Well, I know how he feels. For only this morning, I, too, was struck dumb by a sight not of this world...

...Each year, upon the anniversary of Pearl's death, I make it my habit to return to Lumley and visit the grave of my friend in the churchyard there. After praying to reduce his stay in Purgatory, I then visit Marmaduke at the castle. I play for him and he demonstrates his latest advances in syrups and tonics, and in this way we spend a pleasant evening in each other's company. It was while I was there yesterday, drynking his Aquitaine wine, that he mentioned another Gleeman, one of great renown currently staying nearby at Finchale Priory.

Melchior Blanchflower.

I listened with great interest as Marmaduke telt me the Mercers of Durham had engaged Melchior as entertainment at their annual banquet in honour of their Patron Saint Godric, and that the Sacrist, his Mercer Walter Attwell, and his long-standing former Cellarer, Hugh de Tanfield, would also be in attendance...

...Later that night, as I lay down my head to sleep in Lumley castle, queer vibrations shook my body. Searing heat course't from my heart and travelled to my left shoulder, down my arm, and into my hand. Crying in agony, I thrust the burning appendage out afore me, yet that pain was naught to the inferno which push't into the very tip of my thumb, bursting into blinding whiteness that turned the dark of my chamber to noonday. Sainted light streamed from my thumbnail as I peered into its vertiginous depths and saw the bird flying towards me—a snowy culver more beauteous than aught on Earth. It flew in circles within my nail and spoke with the voice of Saint Godric.

Son, said he. *Come to my tomb at Finchale. Speak with Melchior Blanchflower, for he hath a great and urgent task for thee.*

Godric flew back into my nail—back into me—and I

returned to darkness. What had just happened? Was it Marmaduke's syrup, which I had sampled earlier? Nay, *this* was too powerful. Too pure. I lay in bed, sodden with sweat but filled, also, with a sense of purpose that I confess I had not felt since the passing of my dear Pearl...

98

...The following morn, I did as Godric commanded. I bent a penny in pledge and travelled the single mile from Lumley to the Priory at Finchale, where, two centuries earlier, the noble hermit Godric—once illiterate Pedlar, now hallowed Saint—had tamed that wilde land. Touching Godric's tomb in the chapel, a Monk approach't to whom I requested make my introduction to the famous Gleeman currently in residence.

I found Melchior in high spirits, for he was soon to perform for you all here—the greatest men of this greatest city. Melchior was about my own age, his grey hair receded to a frizzing horseshoe around his bulbous head; a weak jaw hung with multitudinous chins, and a hefty gut—result of a lyftyme's rich eating—housed within the finest apparel.

Sir Blanchflower was befuddled by my appearance, until I put him at ease with a gift of a bottle of Lord Marmaduke's Aquitaine wine. Hearing I was attach't to the noble Lamberts, Melchior accepted the refreshments and we spoke as peers, Gleeman to Gleeman. He telt me of the famous men he had played for as part of King Henry's retinue. And friends, while those tales—the very ones he would hath telt you this night—were legendary, I was more curious to hear of things sunk deeper 'neath tyme's sands. Namely, his days as a bairn at Appleby Castle, and the other lad—son of Gervase the Gleeman—he had known there.

But Melchior did not wish speak of such ancient things. And who could blame him? Why warm thyself with past cinders if thy present burns bright? So I poured him some wine—explaining the tang was due to its rare vintage—and let Melchior continue upon his most favoured theme, that of himself. He carried on until, deep into the bottle, he grutch't of feeling faint. With the quickness of a rain squall, a fever settled upon him and he slip't into a trance the likes of which not even the Finchale Monks, verse't in all matters physikal, could haul him from. As they fuss't about him, it occurred to me that Melchior would no longer be able to fulfil his obligation to you all here, and *this* was the great and urgent task Godric said Melchior had for me. Friends, how could I refuse? Thus, I left Melchior in the care of the Monks, and bent my step towards Durham...

...And, lo, friends, that be almost all. Those of ye whose brains be not churned slop—and that number does not look high—ye may wonder why I was so tardy in my arrival here. After all, Finchale be but a brisk hour's walk. Well, the reason be that, as I took my leave of stricken Melchior, the culver that was Godric appeared once more, but not in my thumbnail. This tyme he sat in a tree by the road.

Mother Naked, said he, *as a pilgrim, I always took the arduous path. For in the long term, does not ease carry a greater burden than difficulty?*

I agree, Godric. But the road to Durham be clear and I have no tyme for diversions.

Tyme? Godric laugh't. *As one who lived one hundred and five mortal years, and now resides Sainted forever, it merries me to hear men speak of tyme. Very well, let me mollify thee. Thy destination still be the Mercer banquet held in my name, but first take the west road which climbs the heugh.*

Godric, I said. *I wish not see that place.*

Son, it may surprise thee! said the Saint, afore taking wing and I saw him no more...

99

...I did as Godric bade. I went west, towards Segerston for the first tyme in forty years. Each step weighed heavier that the last, but I push't onwards and as the land rose, I saw things were, in dede, much changed. The acres which had lain wasted since the Great Pestilence—which Thomas the Bailiff had near ruined us in his attempt to revive—were now sown with endless wheat. I was surprised, also, to see stone walls squaring off one corner of an open field, forming smaller enclosures. Within each grazed a goodly number of sheep, likely belonging to different men. I had seen this done in other hamlets, and not only for livestock, for some folk now grew their own crops in their own fields. But such thoughts fell away when the church spire rose o'er the treeline of the very heugh where I had spent my creeping, cringing youth. And at the sight, bile surged in my throat.

I could scarcely believe it. After a lyf lived in the flux of ever-changing towns and cities, I was now back in the place which had once been my world entire...

...And here, too, things were much altered. The manor house had been rebuilt, its thatch roof replace't by slate tile. Upon the common green, 'neath the oak which once shaded Thomas' increasingly lunatic hallmotes, stood a table laid out with goode meat and ale in honour of Godric. The residents of Segerston buzzed about—many more than in my tyme—and did appreciate mine Gleeman services, for I spent a merry hour playing them happy songs.

During these festivities, I notice't a figure sat upon the edge of things. A man even aulder than I, drooping in a chair. I left off my playing and went to him, for there was something about the fellow I recognised. His clawed hands trembled in his lap, and all o'er did he shake with palsy. Wisps of hair clung to the splotch't egg of his head, and slaver hung from his toothless gob. But the eyes—those eyes were keen. Eyes I knew well of auld.

Greetings, Philip, said I.

When he saw who I was, he let loose a moan.

Da, dread not! called a voice behind me. *It be only a Gleeman.*

I did not mean to fret him, said I, turning to meet the voice, and almost screamed when I did...for the man approaching was the spit of Ralf Deepslough as I had known him.

You did not, said the man. *He hath been thus since apoplexy crippled his speech.*

Saddening to hear, said I, mastering my panic.

Aye, well, it comes to us all in tyme. Edward Deepslough be my name.

Well met, Edward. Sooth to say, I have not pass't this way in decades, and Segerston be greatly changed. Tell me, how long hast you lived here?

Philip gurgled and groaned.

All my lyf, said Edward. *Deepsloughs have been here since tyme out of mind.*

Who now be the Lord's Bailiff?

Edward was befuddled. *Lord's Bailiff?*

And so I learned how, only a fewe scant years after I left, the Bishop of Durham lease't out the church's holdings—Segerston included—to a group of wealthy Merchants. These Merchants then rented out the wasted lands at low price to entice newcomers to the village, dissolving likewise the demesne acres and leasing it to any who could afford it. As a result, labour obligations came to an end and villeins needed only pay a single fee in lieu.

I have seen this change in other places, said I, *but did not think to see it here.*

We become modern at last, laugh't Edward. *My da here, he used to speak of a tyme when the Sacrist had his villeins toil upon his demesne the year round. How they did that, I know not. Now, the fee we pay the Merchants be easy managed, for the tyme saved allows us to work our own lands to greater profit.*

Glad to hear it, Edward. And does it not beg a question?

What question?

Which other iron laws of custom might really be formed of wax?

His perplex't smile shewed he did not understand.

Cry pardon, said I. *Those be the words of an auld friend. Nevertheless, you could leave Segerston if you so wish't?*

Edward's confusion deepened. He look't o'er to the common green, to the sight of Segerston in merriment—eating, courting, dancing, and playing games of quoit and mumblety-peg.

Why would I leave?

A thought came to me.

As a Gleeman, I trade in stories. And I have heard a strange tale concerning this village—the Fell Wraith of Segerston.

Philip shuddered. Edward stroke't his father's wasted arm until he settled.

Aye, we have all heard the stories.

Do you believe them?

They be just stories.

Your da must hath been young then. When he could still speak, did he ever tell of her?

Edward thought a moment. *I did ask him once. For some daft folk still whisper how this Wraith came to our very cottage and killed mine grandparents, uncles, and many others drynking there. They say Da here was the only one to survive, and that he burn't down the auld manor with her in it.*

Thy father did that?

Philip's eyes were hard on mine, and I knew then whose shadow I had seen afore the flames that night. I imagined the auld man as the young man he had been, struggling down the loft ladders with a bellyful of my special ale, shambling past his dead family in pursuit of me. Mayhap he had not been as far gone as he had seemed, or else driven by sheer and blinding rage. How had he set fyre to the manor? A torch toss't into the thatch? Rolled a barrel of pitch from the manor outhouse in through the back door and burn't the place up that way? Whatever had happened, Phillip would be taking the knowledge to his grave, as well he should. All the best tales retain some element of mystery.

And what did he say of those rumours? I ask't. *Thy da, I mean?*

The gurgle in Philip's throat thickened as his son continued.

Only that my family died as rustics die—through sickness

and labour—and the manor burn't because the Bailiff had been a drunken madman.

That was all?

A fly landed on Philip's bald head. Edward brushed it off with a kindness I never witness't Ralf shew his eldest son.

That was all, said Edward. *But then, he was never one for ghost tales...*

100

...And even though a miracle had occurred and I had met a Deepslough I like't, I could not tarry with Edward for tempestuous clouds were gathering to the north. I race't them south to Durham but, as ye saw from my drownded state earlier, I lost that competition. But no matter. All I cared about was getting here and resolving for you the mystery of the Fell Wraith, and the destruction that was visited upon Segerston all those years ago.

So tell me...

...Sacrist...

...Walter...

...Cellarer and gathered Mercers...

...Tell me true, be your curiosity sated...?

...I take as affirmation the collective frothing of your lips. That

be a relief, friends. And as for payment, Sacrist, I shall abide
by thy Clerk's words given when I arrived here wet and tardy,
and informed him I was not Melchior Blanchflower. *Then do
not expect Melchior's fee,* said that lovely fellow. Well, I accept
a lower wage. Actually, Sacrist, I shall ask thy man only for
the coin you gave me that day—a single groat. It changed my
lyf once, and I hope may do so again, for I believe this be my
final performance as a Gleeman. After all, what tale might top
this one? Aye, a single groat seems fitting. The first made me a
Gleeman, and the last makes me *what,* I wonder?

I wonder.

And speaking of Melchior, I know I lack't his refinement
in the telling of this tale. Like the looping gyrations about the
north I took with Pearl, my story hath wandered hither and
yon, but what other way be there to tell it? After all, no single
tale exists sundered from others. Still, I regret if my coarseness as a storyteller hath impeded your enjoyment and failed
to make you see clearly in your imaginings that which I saw.
Mine meagre words, did they conjure the true image of the
Wraith? If only there were some more *certain* way to make you
all see? To cause her appearances afore your very eyes, in this
very hall?

Alas, mayhap this fatal deficiency of communication we all
share—our curse since God tumbled Babel's tower—mayhap
that ought be our final toast?

But does auld Mother Naked also raise a glass? I did
promise myself a cup of wine as reward at the end, did I not?
Well, I refuse. For though I have earned it—God knows I have
earned it—the vintage be not to my taste.

The tang of darnel, friends.

Try as I might, it just does not agree with me.

Not that it hath curtailed your enjoyment. In dede, friends, ye have near sup't it all away! That was what I was about when the Monk found me in the cellars, afore I entered this hall to begin my tale—pouring Marmaduke's darnel syrup into the kegs of wine and ale ye have been drynking all night. Some fifteen large bottles of syrup, carried here in a fardel upon my back—Lord Lambert's entire stock, taken without his knowledge. *Two or three thimblefuls,* that was Marmaduke's warning. *More, and you risk breaking a man's wits eternally.* Well, friends, I should warrant you have drunk far more than a fewe thimb—

LO! Lightening crashes!

The glass't casements shatter inwards!

Rain like blades, wind riving hair and clothes!

And I wonder, friends, what be your hearts seeing at this moment?

That which your eyes wish not...?

...Be it guilt...?

...Fear...?

...*The Wraith...?*

...As my final Gleeman act, allow me to gather up my psaltery and sing you one last verse afore I take my leave—

> *Now ye have heard the end of my tale,*
> *What if ye toss it high on a shelf?*
> *Cast off mine words, let forgetting prevail?*

Best, then, she comes to remind you herself.
She comes for you now
In your cloth of gold,
She comes for you now
In your house of stone,
She comes for you now
In your shuttered wit,
She comes for you now,
Comes for you now,
Comes for you now
Right where you sit.

Acknowledgments

Mother Naked wouldn't exist without the support of many people and organisations. Thank you to Sam Fisher and everyone at Peninsula for believing in the novel, and for helping me write the best possible version of it. Thank you to Jon Gray for the smoking-hot cover. Thank you to my agent Veronique Baxter for her continued faith in my work, and to all at David Higham—I'm eternally grateful. Thank you to Arts Council England and the Society of Authors for the funding which granted me time and space to write a lot of other words before I could write about this strange Durham gleeman. Thank you to Gladstone's library for making me their writer in residence. The month I lived there shaped the book beyond measure, so special thank you to Louisa Yates and Rhian Waller for making me feel so welcome. Thank you to Professor Robert Poole, for the forest walks and vital research recommendations on the pre-Reformation church. Thank you to Kris Philips and Wyn Mason for the beer and writing insights. Thank you to Ann Randall and Jim Bogar for their friendship, and pointers on salting children down for meat. *Diolch* Richard Davis, who lent me his Pembrokeshire home while I finished the book. Thank you to Susan MacDonald for helping me keep writing anything at all. Thank you to my family and friends, for their unwavering support and interest in what I do. A huge thank you to two wonderfully talented writers and friends who provided feedback on early drafts. Thank you, Zakia Uddin. Thank you, Edward Matthews. Their laser-focused edits and discussions showed me how to structure and balance this sinuous tale, while their continued support gave me faith I could do it. I'm constantly inspired by—and learning from—them and their brilliant work. And finally, thank you to my beautiful wife Susan Barker. She is my first reader, greatest friend and champion. Every day, she inspires me to become a better writer and a better person. If I can be considered either of those, it is because of her.